Amid the Ashes

**A CHRISTIAN ROMANCE
SEASONS OF FAITH BOOK 4**

Milla Holt

REINBOK LIMITED
London, United Kingdom

Published by Reinbok Limited, 111 Wolsey Drive, Kingston Upon Thames, Greater London, KT2 5DR

Cover by 100 Covers

Book Layout ©2017 BookDesignTemplates.com

Amid the Ashes / Milla Holt. -- 1st ed.

ISBN 978-1-913416-22-5

Print ISBN 978-1-913416-23-2

WELCOME TO THE MOSAIC COLLECTION

WE ARE SISTERS, A beautiful mosaic united by the love of God through the blood of Christ.

Each month The Mosaic Collection releases one or more faith-based novels or anthologies exploring our theme, Family by His Design, and sharing stories that feature diverse, God-designed families. Stories range from mystery and women's fiction to comedic and literary fiction. We hope you'll join our Mosaic family as we explore together what truly defines a family.

If you're like us, loneliness and suffering have touched your life in ways you never imagined; but Dear One, while you may feel alone in your suffering—whatever it is—you are never alone!

Learn more about The Mosaic Collection at
www.mosaiccollectionbooks.com
Join our Reader Community, too!
www.facebook.com/groups/TheMosaicCollection

BOOKS IN THE MOSAIC COLLECTION

When Mountains Sing by Stacy Monson
Unbound by Eleanor Bertin
The Red Journal by Deb Elkink
A Beautiful Mess by Brenda S. Anderson
Hope is Born: A Mosaic Christmas Anthology
More Than Enough by Lorna Seilstad
The Road to Happenstance by Janice L. Dick
This Side of Yesterday by Angela D. Meyer
Lost Down Deep by Sara Davison
The Mischief Thief by Johnnie Alexander
Before Summer's End: Stories to Touch the Soul
Tethered by Eleanor Bertin
Calm Before the Storm by Janice L. Dick
Heart Restoration by Regina Rudd Merrick
Pieces of Granite by Brenda S. Anderson
Watercolors by Lorna Seilstad
A Star Will Rise: A Mosaic Christmas Anthology II
Eye of the Storm by Janice L. Dick
Totally Booked: A Book Lover's Companion

Lifelines by Eleanor Bertin

The Third Grace by Deb Elkink

Crazy About Maisie by Janice L. Dick

Rebuilding Joy by Regina Rudd Merrick

Song of Grace: Stories to Amaze the Soul

Written in Ink by Sara Davison

Open Circle by Stacy Monson

The Heart of Christmas: A Mosaic Christmas Anthology III

Where Hope Starts by Angela D. Meyer

Flame of Mercy by Eleanor Bertin

Through the Lettered Veil by Candace West

Broken Together by Brenda S. Anderson

Every Star in the Sky by Sara Davison

Where Healing Starts by Angela D. Meyer

All Things New: Stories to Refresh the Soul

Into the Flood by Milla Holt

Through the Blaze by Milla Holt

A Whisper of Peace: A Mosaic Christmas Anthology IV

Twice Sold Tales by Chautona Havig

Within the Storm by Milla Holt

Where Joy Starts by Angela D. Meyer

Every Flower of the Field by Sara Davison

Dancing in the Rain: Stories to Shelter the Soul

Amid the Ashes by Milla Holt

A Thrill in the Air: A Mosaic Christmas Anthology V

Learn more at
www.mosaiccollectionbooks.com/mosaic-books

*To my husband, who is my biggest
cheerleader*

Chapter 1

"YOU WANT TO COME over right now?" Johanna Strand pressed her phone to her ear, her pulse kicking into high gear as she stood at the doorway of her house.

"If you're not busy."

The smooth-as-melted-chocolate baritone on the other end of the phone line belonged to Anton Einarson, the son of her biggest real estate client. "We finally found the missing key to that outbuilding. I wanted to hand it over to you personally, but I'm sitting outside your Havdal office and looking at the closed sign," he said. "So, I need to bring the key to you."

Johanna bit her lip, her stomach doing cartwheels. Of course she'd love to have Anton over. He was attractive and unattached, and she knew her radar wasn't off about the flirtatious vibes he gave off while they worked together. But she was on her way out to meet two of her friends, who were waiting for her to teach them how to make her signature meatball casserole.

Anton's voice slid into her ear. "If you're unavailable, that's fine. I can get you the key some other way, although I know my father wanted the buyer to have it on handover. Plus, I want to put it into your hands myself."

Johanna glanced at the bag of groceries at her feet, her breath quickening. Bethany and Reidun would understand. Being north of forty-five, it was getting harder and harder to meet unattached men who were also gainfully employed, free of bad habits, and reasonably attractive. Plus, of course, she had an obligation to her client. Right? "Sure, I'm free," she said.

"Excellent." The rumble in his voice made her skin tingle. "You said you live near the Berghaven harbor, right?"

"Yes, that's right."

"Text me your address, and I'll see you soon."

She ended the call as her gaze flew over her living room. It should take him about thirty minutes to drive around the fjord from Havdal to Berghaven. Although her robot vacuum kept the floor presentable, the layer of dust she'd been ignoring sprang out in front of her, along with the smudges on her windows. And the bathroom needed cleaning. But half an hour should be enough.

She opened her messaging app and texted her address to Anton.

As soon as he replied with a thumbs up, she stepped toward the kitchen. Her foot brushed against the shopping bags. Oh no, Reidun and Bethany were expecting her right now. She really ought to call to cancel, but explaining would take too long and the minutes were ticking away until Anton got here.

Opening her text app again, she added Reidun and Bethany's numbers to a group message.

Really sorry, but something urgent has come up with a client, and I can't make it today. Can we reschedule? Promise to make it up to you.

Reidun was the first to reply, pinging back in seconds.

Seriously? Your boss better be paying you well. I'll accept your apology only in cupcake form.

Smiling, Johanna picked up the grocery bag and headed to the kitchen. As she set the bag on the floor, her phone buzzed again with Bethany's understanding reply. She had the world's best friends. She knew they'd be okay with her pulling out at the last minute.

There was no time to unpack the grocery bag properly. Not if she was going to make her house presentable.

She grabbed a duster and attacked the coffee table in her living room.

Cleo, her tortoiseshell Norwegian Forest cat, wound herself around Johanna's ankles.

"No time to give you cuddles now, sweetheart," Johanna said. "Company's coming."

She whipped through the house like a whirlwind, flicking away dust and shoving books and papers behind cabinet doors. She cringed as sweat broke out on her forehead. With less than twenty minutes to go until Anton came, she didn't have time for a shower. And the windows needed a spot clean.

Johanna glanced around the room. Perhaps she'd done too much. She didn't want it to look too pristine, because Anton might suspect she'd had to tidy up for his visit. It should look as though she kept a reasonably clean home without having to make any special effort when a guest just happened to drop in. She should mess it up just a tiny bit.

She went to her bookshelf and retrieved the newspaper and book she'd just tidied away, putting them back on the coffee table. Hm, maybe not that paperback romance novel. She picked up the book again, glancing at the couple embracing on its cover. That looked rather lowbrow. Didn't she have a literary tome somewhere?

She replaced *Her Duke's Forbidden Secret* with a beautifully bound hardcover edition of Knut Hamsun's *Under the Autumn Star*. Much better.

Her hand flew up to her head. She'd had a hair appointment a couple of days ago, so her short, dark curls should be okay. But should she change her clothes? Maybe a pair of designer jeans instead of these jogging pants. And if she wore jeans, this T-shirt would have to go, too.

Cleo's green-eyed stare met her when she came back into the living room wearing a different outfit. The cat sat on the purple armchair she'd claimed as her own, her fan-like tail curled around her body.

"Don't look at me like that," Johanna said. "There's nothing wrong with putting my best foot forward."

The doorbell chimed, and Cleo weaved between Johanna's feet as they walked down the hallway.

Anton grinned as Johanna opened the door, his gaze sweeping over her from head to foot and back again.

Her cheeks warmed. Changing her clothes had been a good call. These jeans, bought as a treat to mark a ten-pound weight loss, showed off her trimmed-down physique.

Anton, as usual, was impeccably dressed, his crisp blue shirt setting off his slate gray eyes. "Thanks for letting me stop by. Ooh, what a big cat. Has someone been overindulging in the kitty treats?"

"She's not fat," Johanna said. "She's a Norwegian Forest cat. They're naturally big, and their fur is very fluffy."

"It does look really soft." Anton stooped to touch Cleo's head.

The cat hissed, swiping at his hand with fully extended claws.

Anton leaped back, swearing as Cleo darted past him and out the door.

Heat flooded Johanna's face. "I'm so sorry." She should have warned him not to pet the cat. Cleo often took a sudden dislike to people, especially men. She'd hated every guy Johanna ever dated. "Did she hurt you?"

He examined his hand. Its smooth skin was unbroken. "No, thankfully not."

"Please come in."

He walked past her and into the living room. "Thanks for seeing me. I admit I'm curious about what the home of a hot-shot realtor like you looks like."

"Hot-shot? You flatter me."

"It's the truth." He turned to face her. "Friholmen was languishing on the market for almost two years before you took over our portfolio. My father was very impressed by how quickly you sold it. Between you and me, he thinks you're going places."

He winked, and her stomach fluttered. His father liked her work? "That's very kind of him. But I can't take all the credit. The property sold itself once those updates were in place."

"Don't sell yourself short, Johanna. I like a woman with a bit of ambition." His gaze met hers, jolting her heart rate. "You suggested all the changes. You're far more than an average realtor. There's something really special about you. That's partly why I came by today, besides handing over the missing keys, of course."

Her knees suddenly weak, she sank onto the closest armchair, then mentally kicked herself for forgetting to offer him a seat. Was he going to ask her on a proper date?

Smiling, he lowered himself onto a chair opposite her. "You went above and beyond, and it shows. First things first. Here's the key."

He pulled an envelope out of his pocket, his fingers brushing hers as he handed it over. "My father insists that we offer your agency a quick sale bonus, and he told your boss that a major chunk of it should be yours."

Anton grinned, clearly waiting for a response.

Her heart sank. She'd been waiting for something else. Like an invitation on a date, a question about whether now that they were no longer working together, he'd like to explore a different side to their relationship. Not a pat on the head for her business skills.

She recovered from her disappointment just as his grin began to falter. "Wow, thank you. I'm very grateful. Please pass my thanks on to your father. Like I said, Friholmen practically sold itself. It was a privilege to work with such a wonderful property."

"I'm glad to hear it." He stood, flicking a cat hair off his dark blue pants. "I guess that concludes everything. I'm headed to Bergen on business tomorrow, so this is goodbye."

She took the hand he offered, his grip surprisingly flabby for someone so tall and muscular. "Thanks. Um, safe journey back."

"You're welcome." He glanced around the living room. "By the way, I like what you've done with this place. Down-to-earth, lived-in, shabby chic. Suits you well."

She trailed behind him as he headed toward the door. Passing the kitchen doorway, she glimpsed the grocery bags with the ingredients for the cooking party she'd canceled. She'd given up an evening with her friends so she could get firmly friend-zoned by Anton. Poetic justice.

She waved him off as he headed toward his Jaguar.

A raindrop splashed onto her cheek, and Johanna scanned her porch and front garden. Where was Cleo? Her heart sank as her gaze fixed upon the house next door. Cleo had better not have gone there again.

Sighing, she headed toward her neighbor's house.

Chapter 2

GUNNAR RIKARDSON DROPPED HIS car keys into the bowl next to his front door.

He rolled his shoulders as he walked into the living room. After a day of back-to-back video conferences with his clients, he was looking forward to his evening run along the harbor. He stood in front of the windows, the main reason he'd chosen this house when he moved to Berghaven last year. He never tired of their view of the fjord.

An overcast sky hung over the water. It threatened rain, but that wouldn't stop him from keeping his evening ritual.

His cell phone rang, and he checked the display. It was his sister. That run would have to wait. "Hi, Maria."

"Hi. Is this a good time to talk? I know what you're like with your schedule."

Gunnar stepped closer to the window. "You know I'd drop anything to talk with you."

"You're sure you can squeeze me in between Bible Study and your five-mile run or whatever you're doing at four minutes past six?"

"I'm not that bad. This is the second Thursday of the month, so I've got nothing scheduled until seventeen

minutes to seven." He chuckled. "Seriously, though, what's going on?"

"It's June."

"Yes. And?"

"I'm going to go ahead with the party for Mamma and Pappa's anniversary."

"They've decided to have a party?" Gunnar asked. "I thought they were just going to have a quiet weekend at the cabin."

"Mamma feels relatively well, so they want to do something special. I mean, it's their fiftieth. That's huge. I hope you'll be able to come."

Gunnar sank into a chair. "Is Stefan going to be there?"

"Yes."

"Maria—"

"No, wait. I know what you're going to say. But Mamma and Pappa want all their children at the party. How many people get to celebrate their golden anniversary?"

The room felt stuffy. Gunnar headed to the back door for some fresh air.

As he slid open the French doors, a walking ball of damp tortoiseshell fur swept past him and into his living room. The cat from next door was back. How long had it been waiting out there in this drizzle?

"Gunnar? Are you still there?"

"Yes, I'm here." He sighed into the phone. "Have you told Stefan about your plans?"

"He offered to host the party at his place."

"I see. And did he say anything about me coming?"

The hesitation before she answered spoke volumes. "Um, no. I haven't actually brought it up with him."

Gunnar sighed again, his heart sinking like a stone. "You know I'd love us all to be there if it were up to me. But it might be for the best if I don't attend, especially if Stefan's hosting it. It's supposed to be about Mamma and Pappa, and I don't want to throw a shadow over the event."

"I get it, believe me. And I didn't want to bring this up, but Mamma's been to see the doctor, and the news wasn't great." There was a catch in her voice. "Gunnar, they may not have a fifty-first anniversary. She might not even make it until Christmas. It would mean the world to her—to both of them—to have all her children at this celebration, but I know she's not going to pressure you to come."

Gunnar's fist clenched. It was so unfair. Mamma had fought so hard, suffering through her illness and equally painful treatment so patiently. She never asked for much, and he'd do anything for her. But this might be beyond his power to give. Because of his own actions, he wasn't welcome anywhere near his brother.

"Maybe if I tried to talk to Stefan..." Maria's voice trailed off.

Gunnar sat down, and the large cat instantly hopped onto his knee, its warm weight making it feel like a super-sized fluffy hot water bottle. He

bent forward, touching his forehead to its fur.

"You shouldn't have to mediate between Stefan and me," he said to his sister. "If you push him, it might make things worse. Tell you what—I'll try to reach out to him."

"Thanks. I appreciate that you're trying."

Gunnar had been trying for almost two years, with no results. But he'd try one more time if it meant giving his parents what they wanted for their anniversary.

He ended the call. The cat pushed its large head under his chin, releasing a rumbling purr as Gunnar stroked its silky coat.

He smiled. "You're just a big old softy, aren't you? How'd you know I needed a cuddle?"

The doorbell sounded.

Gunnar sighed. This was the worst time for someone to show up. He wasn't expecting any guests, and he didn't feel like talking to anyone after the load of emotional baggage that now sat on his shoulders. Mamma was dying.

He stood up slowly, setting the cat on the ground as the bell rang again. Whoever was there wasn't in a patient mood.

Gunnar opened the front door.

His neighbor stood there, her brown eyes flashing, arms folded tightly across her chest.

Before he could get any words out, she pointed behind him. "I see you've taken my cat again."

Chapter 3

WHAT WAS IT WITH this guy? Johanna had caught him red-handed, and he didn't even have the sense to look guilty.

Instead, her neighbor stared at her, frowning through his dark-framed glasses. "It was raining and your cat wandered in when I opened the door. I haven't 'taken' it."

Cleo strolled toward Johanna.

"Were you going to bring her over?"

"It's only been here for, like, five minutes. Besides, it's a cat. It goes where it wants."

Cleo settled onto her haunches, staring back and forth between the two humans.

Johanna took a long breath. "Listen, I'm really grateful for what you did for Cleo when she got hurt. But I'd appreciate it if you'd not encourage her to hang out with you. She's getting confused about where she lives. She's an indoor cat, but she's hardly home anymore. She's on medication, and it's really hard to make sure she sticks to the dosage regularly."

"Hey, I don't exactly invite it over. It just seems to show up."

That was something Johanna didn't understand at all. Cleo was a very anti-social cat. The way she'd hissed and scratched at Anton today was how she normally treated all of Johanna's male friends. But for whatever weird reason, this crazy cat was besotted with Gunnar, going over to his house at every opportunity.

"You're not feeding her or anything, right? I already told you about the milk."

"Yes, and I apologized about that. I didn't know cats weren't supposed to have cow's milk, and that was when it first showed up and was all beaten up and I didn't know who it belonged to."

"Well, now you know. Please don't let her in."

He crossed his arms. "Perhaps if your place was better secured, it would have less of a chance to get out and run into trouble and people wouldn't need to rescue it."

Heat flamed Johanna's face. "That was a low blow. Animals have accidents."

He had the good sense to look apologetic. "Sorry. Yes, they do have accidents. And being an animal, if it's really determined to go somewhere, it will."

"She—" Johanna emphasized the pronoun—"will learn her boundaries better if you let her know she's not welcome. I'm not saying squirt her with a water pistol or anything drastic, but please don't let her in."

His face flushed a dark pink. "Noted. I'll make sure to make her feel as unwelcome as possible. You've been reunited now, so if that's all, I have things to do."

He stepped back and closed the door inches from Johanna's nose, leaving her groping, too late, for a killer comeback.

"Come on, Cleo. Let's go home. And you are never to visit that... that man ever again. Do you hear me?"

Cleo cast a disdainful glance at Johanna and strolled back toward home, tail sweeping the air behind her.

Why did everyone around her like Gunnar so much? It wasn't just Cleo, but her best friends, Bethany and Reidun, Bethany's husband Lukas, and their whole group of friends. The man was insufferable. He carried himself like a superior, overly starched know-it-all.

Gunnar had moved to Berghaven last year to work with Bethany's husband. He'd bought the house beside Johanna's early in the spring. Before Gunnar's arrival, Cleo had never shown an interest in the garden next door. Now, she loved to sun herself there, even though Gunnar had made no changes to the place.

Cats were strange.

She needed to take measures to ensure Cleo stopped going to Gunnar's back garden. Perhaps she could build one of those catios to keep the cat confined to her own backyard, but with lots of apparatus so she could get the exercise and stimulation she needed.

It wasn't as though Cleo got either exercise or stimulation at Gunnar's place, anyway. All she seemed to do was stretch out on his porch. And from what she'd seen today, it was clear that Cleo wasn't just doing that anymore. She was also going inside his house.

Gunnar had done her a huge favor, Johanna had to admit, when he'd rushed an injured Cleo off to the vet. They weren't sure what had happened to her, but Gunnar had found Cleo badly hurt shortly before Easter.

Thankfully, Cleo was micro-chipped. When the vet had contacted Johanna, he told her that the cat would have died if Gunnar hadn't brought her straight in for emergency treatment.

Since her recovery, Cleo couldn't seem to stay away from Gunnar's house. Johanna's gratitude was wearing thin, though, as Cleo stayed at his place for longer and longer stretches of time. And Gunnar couldn't seem to understand why Johanna was upset about this. Cleo was her cat, and he had no business confusing the feline.

A catio. That would solve the problem. She'd go online right now and figure out how to install one.

Chapter 4

INSUFFERABLE WOMAN. IT TOOK a huge measure of self-control not to slam the door in Johanna's face.

Gunnar stalked back into his living room. Any other civilized human being would have been grateful to him after he'd found their cat lying injured and close to death and taken it to the vet. But not Johanna Strand. All she did was look down her nose at him and treat him as though he was the Child Snatcher from Chitty Chitty Bang Bang.

What was he supposed to do when the cat sat in the rain and stared at him? Leave it outside?

Through his window, he glimpsed Johanna marching back to her front door with the cat in her arms.

If Johanna thought he was an awful human being for harboring her cat, what would she think if she knew how he'd betrayed his brother?

But he had bigger things to worry about than his neighbor and her petty demands about her cat.

Mamma was dying. And he needed to honor her wish for her fiftieth wedding anniversary. Somehow, he and his brother needed to be under the same roof for the celebration.

Stefan was completely justified in being furious with him. Gunnar knew he didn't deserve his brother's forgiveness, and he couldn't demand that Stefan be okay with Gunnar being at the anniversary party.

But for their parents' sake, Gunnar had to try. Especially after what Maria said about Mamma.

He went to his computer and clicked over to LinkedIn. The professional social media site was the only way Gunnar could keep regular tabs on what his brother was doing. Not in a weird stalker way, but so he could assure himself that Stefan was going from strength to strength in his career.

Gunnar had wrecked Stefan's personal life. Forgiving himself for that was hard enough. He didn't know what he'd do if his actions had led to Stefan's career failure as well.

Gunnar scanned his brother's profile. Seemed that Stefan had earned himself another industry award. Good for him.

Enough procrastinating. It was time to contact Stefan. How should he do it? Calling seemed a bit too intrusive. Assuming Stefan would even talk to him, that is.

An email would be more appropriate. It would give his brother space to decide how to respond rather than putting him on the spot with a phone call.

Which email address should he use? He shot Maria a text, asking for their brother's email. Maria's answer came back almost instantly, and she included Stefan's phone number.

Gunnar typed the email address into his mail client, then stalled as the blank screen stared at him. How should he even start? "Hi Stefan" sounded too breezy and casual, as though they'd spoken this morning rather than two years ago.

But "Dear Stefan" was too formal. Gawking at the blinking cursor would get him nowhere. He needed to write something. He plunged in.

I know you're not expecting to hear from me, but I hope you'll hear me out.

Maria told me about the plans for Mamma and Pappa's anniversary and how much they want all of us there.

I don't expect you to forget all that you have against me, but given how important this is to Mamma and Pappa, I hope you won't be offended if I come to their anniversary party.

Gunnar read what he'd written, then hit the backspace button until he'd deleted every word. It wasn't coming out at all how he wanted. Maybe an email wasn't the way to go after all. It was too easy to misunderstand the written word, since he couldn't convey tone and nuance.

Perhaps a phone call would be better after all.

Lord, let him at least hear me out. He picked up his phone and, steeling his nerves, dialed the number Maria had given him.

The call connected, and Gunnar's heart stumbled at the sound of his brother's voice.

"Hello, this is Stefan Rikardson."

"Hi, Stefan. It's me, Gunnar. I—" He pulled up short as Stefan's voice went on speaking.

"I'm not available to take your call at the moment, but if you leave a message, I'll get back to you at the first opportunity. Speak to you soon."

Heart racing, Gunnar ended the call before the recording alert beeped. He wasn't prepared to leave a message. Without the chance to marshal his thoughts and figure out what to say, that was even worse than composing an email.

He'd try again when he'd thought through what message to leave. But he couldn't do this now. His nerves were shot.

What was he supposed to say? "Hey, Stefan. Listen, I know you're probably still mad at me for stealing your girlfriend, but can I come to the party you're hosting, anyway?"

He bitterly regretted everything he'd done that had caused this rift between himself and his brother, and he'd reached out in every way he could think of to make things right. Stefan had rejected every attempt.

What could he now say? Plead on the grounds that their mother's health was failing and it would mean a lot to her if the family was at least superficially together during this party?

Gunnar stared again at the blank "compose" page of his email client, then buried his face in his hands. It was no use. He couldn't think of any appropriate words to use. Because there were none. What he'd done to his brother was unforgivable.

Chapter 5

JOHANNA SCANNED HER LONG to-do list. Which of these tasks would she have to put aside if she was going to make time to hold her junior colleague's hand through the younger woman's first open house event?

Charlotte stood in front of her desk with a thick document folder clutched to her chest, waiting for Johanna's response.

Johanna drummed her fingers. She had to attend a pre-closing home inspection to make sure the seller kept their word about the negotiated repairs. And there were two closings to coordinate later in the week.

Plus, she was on standby with another client, waiting for them to decide on whether to put in an offer for a home. The deadline for that decision was ten o'clock, and if the buyer chose to go ahead, Johanna would need to move very quickly and get a competitive offer together.

She really didn't have time for anything else today. But, looking at Charlotte's anxious face, she knew she had to make that time.

She remembered what it was like to be just starting out. She'd promised herself to be the mentor she wished she'd had and spare someone else from a painful learning curve.

Her boss, Wilhelm Larsen, didn't pay her any extra for the support she gave her junior colleagues, but Johanna did it anyway.

"How about this?" Johanna said. "I'll have a look at your plan and walk you through the checklist so we can be sure nothing's left out."

Charlotte's features relaxed. "Thank you. When can we do that?"

"Let's see... it's half past seven now, and I have some urgent emails to write. How about right after the stand-up meeting? Quarter to ten?"

Charlotte agreed and walked away, and Johanna turned back to her email. Oh, good, accounts had sent her payslip. It ought to reflect the bonus Anton had mentioned.

She opened the email, zeroing in on the figure on the bottom. The number was roughly the same as usual. No bonus. Maybe it was too early and they would pay the bonus next month. Yes, that had to be it.

She spent the next half hour replying to emails and sorting through photos of properties she planned on listing.

Around her, the office slowly woke up. The scent of coffee hit her nose, telling her that Sigrid, the office manager, was in.

Johanna left her cubicle and went into the common area where the coffee machine stood.

Sigrid, a pleasant-faced woman in her early sixties, looked up at her.

"Morning, Johanna. You're just in time. The coffee is just about ready."

"Morning, and thanks." Johanna filled her cup. "Is Wilhelm in?" She peered over Sigrid's shoulder toward their boss's door.

"Yes, he came in a few minutes ago."

"Nice. I'll go in and have a quick word."

Johanna knocked on Wilhelm's door and waited for him to invite her in.

He was a small, rotund man in his mid sixties with a well-trimmed white beard. He might look like Santa Claus, but the resemblance was only surface-level. He was as tough as flint and just about as easy to wear down.

"Morning, Johanna. Coffee ready, is it? What's going on?"

"I was just about to ask you the same thing. I met with Anton Einarson a couple of weeks ago, and he told me something very interesting."

"Oh?"

Johanna gave Wilhelm a hard look. He was giving nothing away. "He said his father had paid a generous bonus for the quick and profitable sale of Friholmen."

Wilhelm's gaze shifted away. "That's right."

"He said his father asked that I should be paid a significant cut of that bonus. But I just got my payslip and there's no bonus. Is it too early? Should I expect it next month?"

Wilhelm steepled his fingers and finally met her gaze. "Mr. Einarson did give the agency a bonus. But I decide what to do with the money."

Johanna took a step forward, a drop of coffee sloshing out of her cup. "But when we re-negotiated my pay last month, we agreed that I'll get fifty percent of any bonus payments from deals that I close."

Wilhelm rubbed his beard in a show of contemplation. "As I recall, we said you could get up to fifty percent, but I had the final say on exactly how much."

Johanna stared at Wilhelm. He was attempting to revise history right before her eyes. "That's not what we agreed."

"Do you have it in writing?"

Her face flamed. "You were supposed to send written confirmation."

"That's unfortunate. I'll refer you to your employment contract, which spells out all the terms of how bonuses are split. A contract that we actually do have in writing."

"But we were renegotiating my contract." Johanna fought to keep her voice level. "We had a verbal agreement."

Wilhelm shrugged. "We were negotiating, but it wasn't final."

Johanna shook her head. "Wilhelm, you know that bonus is mine."

"Actually, I don't know that. At the risk of repeating myself, your employment contract leaves it at my discretion."

"But didn't Mr. Einarson specifically say the bonus was because of my work, and he intended it to come to me?"

Wilhelm's eyes flickered. "That conversation did take place. But a client cannot dictate how I run my business."

Johanna's grip tightened on her mug. It would probably not be a good idea to dump the contents over Wilhelm's smug face, no matter how tempting. "After all these years and all the hard work I've put in, you're going to do this to me?" She hated how her voice trembled.

Wilhelm rolled his eyes. "Please, no emotional blackmail. You signed a contract and agreed to work on certain terms. If you no longer want to stick to that contract, then..." he gestured toward the door, waving his plump, well-manicured fingers. The light flickered off his diamond-encrusted pinky ring.

She gritted her teeth. "If I don't like it, then I can leave?"

He shrugged, turning back to his laptop.

She stared at him, rage building. Wilhelm remembered every word of their meeting. He had agreed to change the terms of her contract, but had conveniently delayed putting it in writing. That bonus was worth tens of thousands of kroner, and Wilhelm couldn't stand to see the money slip out of his fingers.

"You know what, Wilhelm?" she said. "I just might take you up on that."

His smirk disappeared as he shot his gaze back at her. "What do you mean?"

"I mean I quit. Consider this my two weeks' notice."

His pinky-ringed hand clenched into a fist. "You can't quit."

"Yes, I can. It says so in my contract."

Johanna stalked out of his office, her blood boiling. She set her still-full coffee mug next to the machine.

Of all the things Wilhelm had done—and there had been many—this was by far the worst. She'd slaved away for him for years, hoping that her hard work would pay off. He'd given her raises because it would have looked weird if he hadn't. But he'd flat out refused to increase her commission, because that's where the big money was.

Until a few weeks ago, when she'd finally gotten him to agree to exactly that. And now he was going back on his word.

She was done with Wilhelm. She had some money saved up, thanks to a small bequest her father had left her. It would cover her bills until she found a new job.

She sat at her desk and started to type her formal resignation letter.

Wilhelm appeared at her desk. "Listen, Johanna. Let's not make any hasty decisions. I don't think we've finished exploring all the options."

She swiveled her chair to look at him. "The only option I'm interested in is what we already talked about and agreed to. I'm supposed to get fifty percent of any client-offered bonus."

Wilhelm folded his arms. "Fine. You get fifty percent going forward."

"Not just going forward. I get fifty percent from when we had that first conversation. Which means fifty percent of the Einarson bonus."

"Fifty percent going forward from today. Not including Einarson's bonus."

"No deal, Wilhelm. I'll serve out my two weeks."

He scowled. "Forget the two weeks. Clear out your desk and be out of here by lunchtime."

Chapter 6

WHISPERS BUZZED AROUND JOHANNA as she sat at her desk. Everyone with a pair of functioning ears must have heard Wilhelm's snarled command that she get off the premises by lunchtime.

Out of the corner of her eye, she glimpsed her colleagues filing into Wilhelm's office for the morning stand-up meeting. She squared her shoulders and held her head up. She would not be attending. Wilhelm could explain her absence however he liked.

When the door closed behind the last of her realtor colleagues, Sigrid came over, carrying a cup of coffee in one hand and an empty cardboard box in the other. She glanced over her shoulder at Wilhelm's closed door, then spoke quietly. "Here you go, sweetheart. You didn't finish your coffee earlier, so I brought you a fresh cup. Between you and me, it's high time someone stood up to Wilhelm."

Johanna's eyes filled up as Sigrid put the coffee and box down. "Thank you." Her throat choked up.

Sigrid patted her arm. "Good luck."

Johanna took several slow, deep breaths as the older woman went back to her desk. Why was she getting emotional? She was free of this thankless job and Wilhelm's unreasonable demands. Sigrid was probably one of the few people who was sorry to see her go. The rest of her colleagues would be circling like sharks over her client portfolio, ready to pick off the most lucrative. It stung to think of them profiting off of her hard work.

Then Johanna's conscience pinched her. It didn't matter if her colleagues got the big payoff. Her goal was to serve her clients and to make sure they got the best deal possible when buying and selling their property.

She'd do her best to make it easy for her colleagues to take over her client list. That's what Jesus would do if he were a real estate agent who'd just quit his job, right? Wrap everything up nicely in a bow, even if it meant smoothing the way for Wilhelm himself.

She flipped open a notebook and started a list of handover tasks. She had clients at various stages of the property buying and selling process, and she didn't want to leave any of them stranded. Whoever was taking over her client list would need a clear overview of where things stood. She ought to have had two weeks to manage the transition, but she had just a couple of hours. At least all her files were in good order.

She worked steadily through her list, ticking each item off with a satisfying swish of her pen.

A sound broke her concentration, and Johanna glanced up to see Charlotte staring at her wide-eyed. "Is it true? Did Wilhelm just fire you?"

Was that how Wilhelm was spinning this? A flash of anger ripped through Johanna, threatening her intention to be Christlike. "He didn't fire me. I quit."

"Oh, okay. He told us in the stand-up meeting that you've been terminated for gross insubordination."

Johanna's nails dug into her palms. "Why, that lying—" she caught herself before any more words came out.

Unclenching her fists, she forced herself to take a couple of slow breaths. "That's not what happened. But it doesn't matter now. Either way, I'm leaving." She wouldn't feed the company gossip mill.

"I'm really sorry," Charlotte said. "What are you going to do? For work, I mean."

What was she going to do? Start afresh at another real estate company? She'd spent years cultivating her client list, and the thought of having to do it all over again somewhere else wasn't appealing. The truth was, she didn't love the work enough to make the idea of starting all over again feel exciting.

She shrugged. "I'll figure something out." Thank God for the cushion of her little nest egg.

"I guess that means you can't help me with planning my open house?" Charlotte held up her documents.

Johanna winced. "No. But I'm sure you'll be fine. You know the property inside out, so all you need to do is to be friendly and professional. You've got that down."

"Can I call you if I get stuck or need some advice?" Charlotte gestured with her hand. "You know what they're like around here. Everyone's out for themselves. You were the only one who's willing to help anyone else out."

"You can call and ask for general advice. But I'm not sure it would be appropriate to share any detailed info about clients."

"Okay, I understand. Well, good luck with everything." Charlotte gave her a quick smile, then walked away.

Johanna worked steadily through her list with no further interruptions.

Nobody else stopped by her desk to say hi or wish her well.

As the clock ticked toward one PM, she began to feel a weight lifting off her shoulders. She was free of this place. Free of Wilhelm's unreasonable demands and of the hyper-competitive piranha tank environment he bred. And she wouldn't miss the forty-five minute commute around the fjord from her home in Berghaven.

She was ready to do something different. Something fun. A message pinged through on her phone, and she glanced at her screen. It was an alert from her bank, telling her she'd just received a transfer of funds. The payment was for ads that ran on her

YouTube cooking channel. A pretty decent chunk, too.

As she stared at the message, an idea began to form in her head. Maybe, just maybe, she could leave the real estate business entirely behind her and move on to something else.

Johanna stood at the doorstep of her friend Bethany Meland's house, each hand grasping a plastic grocery bag.

Her arms ached from lugging the contents of her desk out to her car earlier that afternoon, but it was a good kind of tired. Spending the evening with her friends was exactly what she needed.

Bethany ushered her in. "Great to see you. Reidun's here already, and we're eager to start."

"Thanks. I'm really sorry about bailing on you last time. But today, you'll learn all the secrets of my signature meatball recipe."

Bethany gave her a hug. "I can't wait! Let's go through to the kitchen."

Reidun Norberg leaned against the kitchen island, nursing a cup of coffee. "How's your day been?"

Johanna paused for a moment, glancing at each of her friends in turn. "Intense, actually. I quit my job."

Reidun and Bethany exclaimed in unison, but Bethany's voice came out loudest. "No way! When did this happen?"

"This morning."

"And you're just telling us now? Why did you quit?"

"Wilhelm," Johanna said.

Reidun rolled her eyes. "It's about time. I'm surprised you've stuck with him this long. What finally pushed you over the edge?"

"It's a long, boring story. But to cut it short, at my last performance appraisal, I got Wilhelm to agree that if a client offered us a quick sale bonus, I'm supposed to get at least fifty percent of it. Earlier this month, a client paid the agency a bonus, mentioned me by name as the reason why they were so happy, and told Wilhelm I should get the bonus. I found out that Wilhelm pocketed it and wasn't going to tell me."

Bethany stared at her open-mouthed. "What? But didn't he agree to the fifty percent thing?"

"I stupidly never got that in writing."

Bethany groaned. "Oh, no."

"Wait." Reidun held up a hand. "How did you find out about the bonus? Did the client tell you?"

"His son did. If it wasn't for Anton, I'd be in the dark about all this."

Reidun raised an eyebrow. "Anton, huh? You're on a first-name basis with this son?"

A rush of heat flooded Johanna's face. "He's a nice guy."

"I see," Reidun said. "Well, I'm glad you've given Wilhelm the heave-ho, but what are you going to do for work now? You don't look too upset about it."

"That's because I'm not." Johanna laughed. "Call me crazy, but I'm more excited than anything. I'm really blessed because I don't have to start job-hunting immediately, thanks to what my dad left me. So, I thought this might be the perfect time to make a go of my online cooking thing."

Reidun and Bethany exchanged glances.

"O...kay," Reidun said. "How exactly do you get an income from that? I mean, don't get me wrong—your Instagram and YouTube stuff is really fun to watch and I've learned so much from your cooking tips, but I thought it was just a hobby."

Johanna pointed at her friend. "See? This is why I tell you stuff. You're guaranteed to poke holes into my boat before I jump in and sink."

"Hey, sorry if I'm being a wet blanket. I just like to be practical."

"I'm just kidding." Johanna squeezed Reidun's arm. "That's exactly why I wanted to run this by you. You always think things through so thoroughly that by the time anything passes your approval, it's got to be solid."

Reidun blushed. "You flatter me, but thanks. So, what's your money-making plan?"

"There are a few income streams I could work on. I'm already getting money from YouTube every time a company shows ads during one of my videos. It's easily enough to pay my car note every month."

Bethany's eyes widened. "Whoa, that much? That's incredible."

"Thanks. And that's without even really trying. I figure if I put my mind to it, I could grow my subscriber base even more. If I build up a following, I could get brands to sponsor my channels. There are people who are making millions doing this kind of thing, and I don't mean big celebrities, either. Just regular people making content about things that interest them."

"If you say it's possible, I believe you," Reidun said.

Bethany nodded. "Sounds like you have something of a plan."

"Actually, I don't." Johanna scrunched her face. "Not a solid one, anyway. I just have a few vague ideas. I was hoping Lukas might be able to help me out. Isn't that the kind of thing he does? Help small businesses do planning and stuff and figure out how to become successful?"

"Sort of," Bethany said. "But he's more of a productivity coach. I'm not sure whether he could do the kind of thing you need, but you could ask him yourself. Actually, he's home right now. I'll see if he's free to answer some questions."

Bethany left the room and came back a couple of minutes later, followed by her husband, Lukas.

Johanna always felt a sweet ache in her heart when she saw them together. Would she ever find a man who adored her as much as Lukas loved Bethany? She'd failed so far, and it wasn't for lack of trying. But Bethany deserved her happily ever after with all she'd been through.

Lukas walked forward with a smile. "What's this about you quitting your job and hoping to make a living with your online hobby?"

Johanna leaned forward, resting her elbows on the kitchen island. "Could you give me some sort of training or coaching so I can start things off, right?"

"I like how you're thinking," Lukas said. "But that kind of coaching isn't exactly in my wheelhouse. I help people who work within a corporate structure to streamline their business processes and use their employees' strengths more effectively. What you need is someone whose specialty is in helping small businesses and startups. Because that's exactly what you are—a very small business who's just getting started."

Johanna's heart sank. "So, you can't help me?"

"I could try, but I wouldn't be the best fit for what you need. But I know someone who would be."

Johanna brightened. "Who?"

"Gunnar Rikardson."

Her heart was back in her boots. Gunnar! Of course, he and Lukas worked together, but it hadn't crossed her mind to think of what exactly he did. "Oh."

"His area of expertise is in small businesses," Lukas said. "That's why he's such a great fit as my business partner. I work with bigger companies, and he helps smaller ones, as well as people who are solo-preneurs. I've seen him do some amazing work, and his testimonials are brilliant."

Johanna crossed her arms. There was no polite way to put her misgivings into words, especially since Lukas and Bethany loved that annoying neighbor of hers so much.

Reidun spoke up. "I'm not sure that Gunnar and Johanna are exactly *simpatico.*"

Lukas looked at her, eyebrows flying up. "Why on earth not?"

"It's a long story." Johanna waved her hand to shut Reidun up. "But, yeah, I don't know whether that would work. Can you think of anyone else who could help me?"

"Off the top of my head, there are two whom I'd be comfortable recommending. Maybe three at a stretch. But, honestly, Gunnar's the guy I'd go with. In fact, he's *my* consultant."

Johanna held up her hand. "Hang on a moment. You're a business consultant, but you need a business consultant?"

"Absolutely. He helps give me clarity when I can't see the wood for the trees. I think most good consultants see the value in getting their own business or personal coaching."

"Okay," Johanna said. "Then tell me who Gunnar's coach is, and I'll hire that guy instead."

Her friends laughed at her light tone, but Johanna was only semi-joking.

Lukas said, "Seriously, though, I'd consider working with Gunnar if I were you. Check out his testimonials if you're worried. You could even call one of his clients and get their take on what it's like to work with him."

"No, if you say he's good, I believe you. I'm just not sure he'd be good for me." Johanna pointed at her chest.

Reidun crossed her arms. "Isn't it worth a try, though, Johanna? You don't have to be best friends with him or anything. He's got the expertise you need, and he lives right next door. Both of you are grownups and professionals. It just seems like too good an opportunity to waste."

Johanna grimaced. The guy had slammed the door in her face the last time she'd talked to him. Not exactly what she considered grownup or professional. But was she letting her ego get in the way of her best interests?

She needed this business to work. What she was making right now wasn't enough to cover all her living expenses, and her savings wouldn't last forever. And if she couldn't get this business off the ground, she'd need to find a job again. Not an easy thing to do in her late forties in this small town. An image flashed in her mind, of her having to go back to Wilhelm to beg for her old job back.

If Gunnar really was her best option to help her get on the right track, she'd better swallow her pride and approach him. It'd only be for a short while.

She sighed. She was a good cook. Surely she could come up with a dish that could make humble pie somewhat edible. "Okay, I'll give Gunnar a go. But, Lukas, would you mind asking him for me? We didn't part on the friendliest of terms last time we spoke."

Lukas's eyebrows flew up. "I have questions... but I'll let it rest. I'll ask him when I see him tomorrow. I think you're making the right decision."

Chapter 7

GUNNAR STARED AT HIS cellphone. He was doing this for Mamma. It was just a phone call. Only a few words.

His drafts folder had several emails to his brother he'd started and discarded without sending. None of them felt right. It would be better to call. What was the worst that could happen? Stefan hanging up on him? And if he did hang up, then at least Gunnar would know that he'd tried, and he could take that off his conscience. A conscience that was already weighed down with so much that he could never undo.

He dialed his brother's number, and the now familiar message played into his ear. Stefan's voice, sounding professional and friendly. This time Gunnar didn't hang up, but waited for the beep.

When it sounded, he waited a heartbeat before he spoke. "Hi, Stefan. This is Gunnar. I, um, hope you're well. Maria told me about Mamma and Pappa's anniversary party and how they want both of us to be there. But I'm not going to show up unless you're okay with it. Could you please let me know whether you're okay with that? Or maybe pass the message on to Maria. Thanks. Bye."

He ended the call, the phone slick with sweat from his palm. That voicemail was awful. Maybe he should have deleted the message and done it again to make it sound better. Smoother. More likely to move Stefan.

He sighed just as his business partner, Lukas Meland, rapped on the door frame of his office and walked inside.

"Anything the matter?" Lukas asked. "That was one huge sigh."

Gunnar shook his head. "Just family stuff. What's up?"

Lukas dropped into a chair in front of Gunnar's desk. "I've got a favor to ask. You know Johanna, right? Bethany's friend. Of course you know her; you live next door to her. But your face tells me whatever beef she has with you, the feeling is mutual."

"What expression is on my face? And what favor is this?" Gunnar thought for a second, then groaned. "No, wait, please don't tell me you've set me up on a date with her or something insane like that."

Lukas laughed. "A date? That was the farthest thing from my mind. But clearly not from yours. Hmm... what's going on here?"

Gunnar wadded a piece of paper into a ball and hurled it at his friend. It hit Lukas in the chest, only making him laugh harder.

Still chuckling, Lukas raised both hands. "No, I haven't come to suggest a date with her. Although now that you mention it, she's single and lovely, and you're single and reasonably attractive. Hey, okay, I'll stop now! Put your ammo away. Seriously, though, it's about business. Her business. She's got this side hobby as a social media chef, and she wants to make it into a full-time thing. She's looking for a business coach. I said she should hire you, and she asked me to approach you on her behalf."

Gunnar folded his arms. This wasn't making any sense. "We're talking about Johanna, Bethany's friend. And you say she wants to hire me? *Me*? Are you sure about that?"

"She said it herself. Listen, I don't want to be the buffer between you guys, or whatever. I won't even ask what's going on. I'm just passing on a message. Except... what's going on?"

Gunnar laughed. "So much for not asking. But I have no problem telling you because it really is ridiculous. So silly I never even thought it was worth bringing up to you because then I'd look foolish. Her cat likes to hang out at my place, and she doesn't like that."

"Is that all?"

"I know, right?" Gunnar shrugged. "That's all. But it's built up into this cold war situation. The last time we talked, I might have shut the door in her face."

"That's not good. No wonder she's not keen on working with you. Anyway, since you don't want to take her on as a client, I'll just let her know." Lukas pushed back his chair and stood.

"Who said I don't want to?"

"Wait, what, you do?"

"No, I don't," Gunnar said. "But I didn't say that yet. I'll be reasonable and hear you out."

"That's it, really. She's quit her job and wants to spend some time building up this business of hers. She's got a cushion of a few months to make it work before she'll have to find another job. I think her best chance is if she gets someone to help make sure she's focusing on the right things."

Gunnar sighed. This was exactly the kind of project he loved doing. Beyond the good living he made out of it, he loved helping people turn their passion into their living. There was no feeling like it.

But could he really work with the crazy cat lady? She'd already shown herself to be unreasonable.

On the other hand, Lukas and Bethany were his closest friends. And Bethany was very close to Johanna. For their sake, he'd make an effort to put aside his personal feelings and help Johanna build her business. He could be a detached professional. If he failed to work with her, it wouldn't be his fault.

"Fine. Tell her to call the office and make an appointment."

Chapter 8

GUNNAR CLENCHED HIS FIST as, yet again, his call to Stefan went to voicemail. Surely, two days was enough time for his brother to retrieve his messages?

He must have called ten times since his first attempt, trying at different times of the day. The result was always the same. The phone call connected and the voicemail message would kick in.

He ended call number eleven. There was no point in leaving another voicemail. Maria would have told him if Stefan was on holiday or somehow out of cellphone range. He should have been able to answer his phone by now, or at least received the multiple voicemails Gunnar had left.

Unless... a sneaking suspicion entered Gunnar's mind, curling into his thoughts like a wisp of noxious smoke. Was Stefan blocking his calls? There was one way to find out.

He stepped out of his office and headed to the front room of the house. As he walked through the door, he called out to the young woman who doubled as receptionist and PA for him and Lukas.

"Hey, Inger-Britt, could you do something for me?"

She glanced up, a flush of pink spreading over her cheeks as her face lit up. "Yes, of course."

Gunnar groaned inwardly. Why did Inger-Britt look at him like that? He wasn't blind. She was a lovely girl, and she was sending all the right signals. A wayward corner of his mind registered how attractive she was, with her limpid blue eyes and wavy brown hair. But he knew what lay down that road, and it was nothing good. And it wasn't just that she was about twenty years too young for him.

She sat up straighter, tucking a strand of hair behind her ear. "How can I help?"

"Could you do me a favor and call this number for me?" He grabbed a pen and sticky note from her desk and jotted down the digits he now knew by heart. He misjudged the distance and his fingers stumbled into hers as he pushed the note toward her.

Inger-Britt's blush deepened. "Sure. What shall I say?"

Was she actually batting her eyelashes? Gunnar crossed his arms. "I want to know whether it goes to voicemail. If it does, hang up straight away. If someone answers, just apologize for bothering them."

"Okay." She reached for the office phone.

Gunnar held up his hand. "Use your mobile, please."

She blinked at him. "My—all right."

Gunnar paced in front of her desk as she tapped in the number and held the phone against her ear.

A moment later, she said, "Oh! No, I'm really sorry to bother you. Goodbye." Putting the phone down, she turned her gaze to Gunnar. "The call went through. He said his name was Stefan Rikardson."

Stefan had blocked his phone number. Back in his office, Gunnar sank into his chair. He'd suspected something was up, but now he knew it for sure. No wonder all his calls had gone to voicemail no matter what time of day he tried to reach Stefan.

How was he supposed to mend fences when his brother was blocking his calls? He pushed his hand into his hair.

Stefan had every reason to cut Gunnar out of his life. It was he, Gunnar, who had done the unthinkable, and now his whole family was paying the price.

His hands balled into fists, and he slammed them against his desk, causing a pile of paper to slide onto the floor just as someone knocked on his door.

Johanna, the cat lady, stepped in, her glance running over his face and the papers fluttering downward. "I'm sorry. Is this a bad time? I thought we had an appointment at ten o'clock."

Heat searing his face, Gunnar stood. "No, we do have an appointment. I was expecting the receptionist to tell me when you got here. Give me a moment to grab these."

He stooped to pick up his papers.

Johanna stepped around a stray brochure and sat on the edge of a chair. "I came in with Lukas, so I guess that's why she didn't call you."

Gunnar stacked the papers back onto his desk and put a snow-globe on top of them to act as a paperweight. He faced Johanna. "Apologies for the delay. What can I do for you?"

She shifted in her seat. "Did Lukas tell you anything?"

"He mentioned a couple of things, but I'd rather hear it from you." After that awkward start, Gunnar wanted to be in the driver's seat for this meeting. Johanna was on his home turf now.

"Um, okay." Her words came out quickly, and she was one of those people who talked with their hands.

"Well, um, I'm not sure how much you know, but I'm a self-trained chef. I love cooking and taking pictures and videos of what I make, and that's how my YouTube channel started."

Gunnar had his pen poised over his notepad. "How many years have you been making videos?"

"I don't know. Maybe ten or so."

"How many subscribers do you have now?" He scribbled on his notebook.

"Something like seventy thousand."

"And what's their engagement rate like?"

Johanna blinked at him. "Engagement rate?"

"You don't know what that is?"

She shook her head.

"That should be fairly straightforward to check." He made another note. "And how much did you make over the last twelve months, before and after expenses?"

Her gaze slid away from his. "I guess by expenses you mean things like equipment and things I use while making my content? It's hard to say, because I feel like these are things I'd be buying, anyway, like kitchen gadgets and ingredients. But I get about $700 on the low end. That's about, what, 7,500 kroner? My best month ever, I got $1,200. I keep the accounts separate and I report it at tax time, so I can check the records and let you know."

Gunnar wrote the numbers down. If Johanna was accurate, that was impressive for someone who was just doing this as a hobby. Her business clearly had potential. But it took more than potential to succeed as a solo entrepreneur. Before he wasted her or his time, he intended to find out whether Johanna had the grit and drive to make it.

"Let's talk about your other social media accounts. Do you have a presence anywhere else apart from YouTube?"

She brightened, as though she were on more solid ground. "I have an Instagram account and a Facebook page. I've also got a blog."

"Do you have any numbers for those? Followers on Instagram and Facebook? Engagement stats? Traffic numbers for your blog?"

She crossed her arms and shook her head, her body curling inward.

Gunnar drummed his fingers on his desk. The picture was getting clearer. "You want this to become your primary source of income. How much do you need this business to earn every year?"

"I don't know." She shrugged. "I don't need that much—my house is paid off, so I don't have a mortgage or anything. Off the top of my head, maybe 300,000 kroner a year."

Gunnar nodded. "And my understanding is that you have a limited timeframe to lay the groundwork for this. How long do you have until you would need to get a new job, if you're unable to build up the business?"

"A year or so, at a stretch."

He put his pen down. "So, let me get this straight. You don't know what your business costs are, but you have a vague idea that it's at least paying for itself. You're unfamiliar with what engagement means. You're not clear how many subscribers or followers you have on any of your social media channels. You can't tell me what your blog traffic is like. But you hope that in the course of a year, you'll be able to earn 300,000 kroner worth of profit out of this business venture. Am I correct so far?"

A dark pink flush tinged her tawny cheeks. "Yes."

"Okay." He leaned back in his chair. "Normally when a client comes to me, they've got a handle on the most basic indicators of where they stand at the moment. As a small business owner, you're going to have to be on top of this information. You'll need to have it right at your fingertips, or at least know where to look for it."

She pressed her lips tightly together as he spoke, the color in her cheeks deepening.

Gunnar picked up his pen again and started to write on his notepad. "Before we go any further, I'll give you some homework so that you can take a snapshot of where your business stands right now. It'll be helpful to me, but it's primarily for your benefit. These are things you should know well before you can have a productive discussion about your business. First of all, find out how many subscribers you have on your YouTube channel.

Check the engagement rate on the last three months of content. I'll show you how to do that—it's not that hard. And, finally, look up your traffic stats on your blog and on all your social media accounts."

He glanced at her. Her hands were balled into fists on her lap.

"You might want to take some notes," he said. He turned back to his own notepad. "So, that's the first thing. Traffic and subscriber numbers. Second, you'll need to look into your financials and get a ballpark figure of how much you're making, and what your costs are. When you've got all that baseline information, we can schedule another meeting and really get down to work."

He looked up at her again. "You didn't write any of that down. Would you rather I send you an email summarizing what I need from you?"

She shook her head, getting to her feet. "Thanks for your time, but I can tell this isn't going to work."

What was with this woman? "Excuse me?"

"This." She waved her hand, flapping it back and forth between them. "I don't think I can work with you."

"What? Because I'm asking you to do some homework and gather basic business information?" He should have known she would be trouble.

"Because of your attitude." She placed her hands on her hips. "Fine, maybe I don't know what I'm doing, and I should have got all that data before I came. But you're condescending and clearly have no respect for me. You were looking down your nose at me the minute I walked in here. I'm not claiming to be an expert on all of this. If I were, I wouldn't need a coach. Maybe my expectations were wrong, but in any case, I think we're done here. What do I owe you for your time?"

Gunnar was sure his face was as red as hers. It felt like it was bathed in flames. He kept his voice even. "If that's how you feel, then perhaps it's best not to work together. I give a free initial consultation, so there'll be no charge. Good luck in your future endeavors. I look forward to hearing of your success."

She glared at him, then walked out of his office. She even managed a flounce with her swirly skirt.

Gunnar slammed his fist on his desk. Why had he let Lukas talk him into this? That went about as badly as it could have possibly gone. But what was he expected to do when someone showed up as unprofessional and unprepared as Johanna? There was no way she would succeed as an entrepreneur with that type of approach.

Had he been extra hard on her because of their earlier disagreements? He'd gone out of his way to be clinical and professional. But based on his interactions with her over that cat, he should have known she wouldn't be reasonable.

Good riddance. He had more important things to worry about than Johanna Strand and her half-baked business idea.

Chapter 9

STUPID, BURNING, UNSHED TEARS stung Johanna's eyes as she left Gunnar's office.

Why had she opened herself up to this? She'd known that working with him was a bad idea. He'd clearly relished the chance to let her know how incompetent he thought she was.

So what if he had a point about how unprepared she'd been coming into the meeting? She didn't know all this stuff—that's why she needed a business coach. Her social media chef gig was just a fun hobby, and she didn't expect to be shamed by the person who was supposed to be helping her transition it into a business.

She climbed into her car and slammed the door. Did entrepreneurs spring fully formed from their mothers' wombs, or did everyone have to learn the ropes at some point?

Gunnar was way out of line. She couldn't understand how he'd gathered all those glowing testimonials. Or, for that matter, how a guy like him was even such good friends with Bethany and Lukas.

A truck honked and flashed its lights as Johanna cut it off at a junction. Great, now she was being a jerk on the road. She needed to calm down before she caused a wreck. *Breathe slowly, and count to ten.*

She eased up on the gas. Gunnar may have made her feel like an idiot, but he would not cost her her nice new Audi. She kept under the speed limit for the rest of the ten-minute drive home.

Walking up to her front door, she was still stewing over Gunnar's every word and gesture. The way he drummed his fingers as he watched her squirm.

"These are things you should know before you consider making this a full-time business," she muttered in a whiny, nerdy voice. Fine, it was childish to mimic him and he sounded nothing like that, but it made her feel better.

Good luck with her future endeavors, indeed. She'd show him. She slammed the front door behind her.

Cleo stood in the hallway, looking up at her.

Johanna scooped up the cat, burying her face in her warm flank. "Sorry about slamming the door."

Cleo allowed herself to be held, curling up as Johanna sank onto an armchair.

"That friend of yours is a real jerk," Johanna said. "I have no idea what you see in him. You are not to go back there. Do you hear?"

Her cellphone rang, and Johanna reached for her purse. What? Anton was calling. Her heart did a tap dance. She fumbled for the answer button before the voicemail could kick in. "Hi!"

"Hi, Johanna. Are you free to talk for a minute?"

"Sure." Did she sound breezy and casual enough? "What's on your mind?"

"My father called your office to discuss our portfolio and expected to speak with you, but they told him you'd left. That must have been sudden."

"Yes, we parted ways last week."

"I'm sorry to hear that. Could I ask why?"

Johanna hesitated. It wouldn't be professional to tell Anton all the gory details of why she'd resigned. A toned down explanation would be best. "Wilhelm and I couldn't agree on what amounts to a fair split of client bonuses."

"Ah." His baritone rumbled through the phone, making her ear tingle. "Did it have anything to do with the bonus my father paid out?"

"That was only the latest trigger in an ongoing debate."

Anton sighed. "I feel terrible about that, Johanna, and I wish there was something I could do. Could I at least buy you lunch today? If you're not busy, I mean."

Her heart soared. "No, I'm not busy. Lunch would be wonderful."

"Excellent. Shall we say the Havdal Country Club at one o'clock?"

"Sounds good. I'll see you there."

Johanna ended the call and got to her feet, setting Cleo on the floor.

The cat stared up, swishing her fan-like tail.

"Sorry, Cleo, I've got to get ready. What should I wear to a country club lunch?"

Just when her morning seemed like a disaster, things had taken a sharp turn for the better.

Johanna hoped she wasn't over-dressed as she walked through the doors into the Havdal Country Club. Half her wardrobe lay strewn around her bedroom, but this pale pink mid-calf-length dress had won. Its wrap-around style flattered her waist, and she hoped the filmy skirt swung gracefully as she walked.

Anton stepped forward, hand extended, looking like a business casual magazine spread in a crisp blue shirt and tan slacks. "Good to see you." His gaze traveled down her body. "Call me old-fashioned, but I think women always look best in dresses, don't you?"

Johanna did a lightning quick mental inventory of her wardrobe. She'd better get herself some more feminine clothes.

He leaned downward, grazing her cheek with his lips.

She resisted an impulse to press her hand against the side of her face.

"I believe our table is ready," he said.

A tall maître d' ushered them into the half full dining room, and several female gazes tracked Anton as he led the way to their table.

The waiter seated them with a flourish.

Anton smiled at Johanna. "I told my father you're no longer working with Wilhelm. He's happy to transfer our portfolio to you, whichever real estate firm you decide to work with."

Johanna's heart galloped. "Wow, that's very generous of him, and I'm very touched. But I'm not going to continue in real estate, at least not for the immediate future. I'd like to try something else."

The elder Mr. Einarson's offer was a soothing balm to her ego, especially after the battering it had received from her meeting with Gunnar. At least someone believed she was a competent professional.

"You're leaving real estate?" Anton stroked his chin. "What exactly are you going to do now?"

She hesitated, reluctant to tell him what she was up to after Gunnar had poured so much scorn on her abilities as an entrepreneur. "I have a moderately successful hobby as a social media chef and influencer. I want to turn it into a full-time business."

He stared at her over the rim of his water glass. "Oh? You are full of surprises. A social media influencer? Where can I find your content?"

She gave him her YouTube handle. "That's my main hub, but I also have a lot happening on Instagram and my blog."

"Hold on a minute while I look you up." He pulled out his cellphone and tapped on the screen.

Johanna did her best to hide her anxiety while Anton scrolled for about a minute.

He looked up, flashing her a smile. "This looks very professional. You say it's only a hobby? I love your titles and your aesthetics. And it looks like you get a decent number of views, too. How long did you say you've been doing this?"

"Ten years. But only seriously for about three years. That's when it started making some money."

He turned back to the screen. "You've got a good amount of content with that cat of yours, too. People love cats online, for some reason."

"Cleo always brings in lots of views," Johanna said.

"I can see how this could be a viable business. You're a woman of many talents, Johanna Strand."

The way he said her name made her shiver. "Thank you."

"I'd like to help any way I can. Some of my associates like to sponsor social media influencers as part of their marketing strategy. Do you use sponsors or paid partnerships?"

"No. Not yet, anyway. But I'd be open to that if the right opportunity presented itself."

He grinned. "That's exactly what I like to hear. I admire a woman who's ready to get out there and make things happen."

Johanna's face flamed as he stared into her eyes. Was he flirting with her?

He tapped his finger against his chin. "To start with, I'm especially interested in your current traffic numbers, subscribers, engagement rates, and your projected growth. Could you mail me your business plan? I'd love to see where you aim on taking this."

Those blasted stats again. "Okay." Johanna nodded, hoping her voice didn't sound like she'd just learned about engagement rates today. And what even was projected growth? Anton didn't need to know she had no business plan.

"Excellent. Email it to me as soon as you can. But shall we enjoy our lunch? I've got a meeting at half-past two."

He motioned for the waiter, who was hovering just out of earshot.

Johanna's mind was reeling. She loved the way Anton looked at her now that he thought she was a smart entrepreneur. She had so much to do. The kinds of things Anton had asked for were exactly the info Gunnar wanted. But Anton treated her as a professional while Gunnar behaved as though she were a clueless halfwit. She'd better get a business plan together before Anton changed his mind about her.

Chapter 10

"Is Johanna gone already?" Lukas poked his head around his friend's office door at the end of the day. "Do you think you can help her?"

Gunnar looked up from his screen, meeting Lukas's gaze. It was time to face the fallout. "You mean she hasn't told you? I thought word would have got around by now. It went more or less like I warned you it would."

Lukas frowned, stepping into the room. "What, you mean it didn't go well?"

"Let's just say Ms Strand decided she didn't require my services."

"So she's not going to be your client?"

"Nope."

"What went wrong?"

"You really haven't heard anything?" Gunnar asked. He'd imagined Johanna would have gone straight to Bethany, who would have filled Lukas in on the disastrous meeting.

Lukas shook his head. "Not a word, and I talked to Bethany earlier. Now you've got me worried. Was it that bad?"

"I told her I needed some information about her business, and I guess she didn't like my tone."

"Your tone? What does that mean?"

Gunnar ran through his conversation with Johanna in his mind. Her words came back. She'd stood in exactly the same spot where Lukas stood now, her brown eyes flashing. *You're condescending and clearly have no respect for me.* He shifted uncomfortably.

Lukas folded his arms. "Gunnar, what did you say?"

"Look, she came in completely unprepared, okay? I treated her like a grown adult who needs to be on top of her game, rather than a child looking to be spoon fed. I asked her for some details about her business. You know, the usual key indicators. Subscribers, followers, engagement rates, last twelve months' revenue. She didn't have any of that information, and I told her she needed to know those things before we could go any further. She said she can't work with me, and she basically fired me."

Lukas pinched the bridge of his nose with a sigh and a shake of his head.

Gunnar responded to the unspoken rebuke. "If she wants to succeed as an entrepreneur, she needs to treat her work as a business instead of a casual hobby. I was trying to get her to see that."

Lukas stared at Gunnar for a long moment. Finally, he stepped toward the door. "This isn't like you. I know you don't sugarcoat things, and maybe you had a point. But there's a line between telling it like it is and being straight up rude and confrontational. I wasn't here and I can't tell exactly what went on between the two of you, so I'll hold off on the long lecture. If you truly believe, hand on heart, that you handled this well, then fine. But if not, I hope you'll make it right, especially since both of you are my friends."

Gunnar watched Lukas walk out of the office. He wished his conscience would allow him to dismiss what his friend had said. If Johanna had come to him as a stranger off the street, asking him about her business, would he have handled the meeting in exactly the same way? *You're condescending and clearly have no respect for me. You were looking down your nose at me the minute I walked in here.*

His gaze went to his computer screen and the Bible text he used as his desktop wallpaper.

"Search me, O God, and know my heart: try me, and know my thoughts, and see if there be any wicked way in me, and lead me in the way everlasting."

These verses had helped bring him to his senses after the madness with his brother's girlfriend. They were the daily prayer he relied on to help him keep him from straying again.

Did he dare ask God to examine his heart about his meeting with Johanna?

Gunnar sighed. Lukas was right. And what was worse, Johanna was right, too. He had been rude to her. On paper, what he'd said to her was correct. She did need that information in order to move forward with her work. But he'd enjoyed pointing out her deficiencies a bit too much. No matter how unfocused and scattered her plans were, he should have shown her more respect.

Okay, Lord, I'm sorry for acting like a jerk.

He should probably call Johanna and apologize. He reached for his phone, then caught the time. It was already after six, and he needed to grab some groceries, make himself some dinner, and catch an online seminar that was beginning at eight. He'd call Johanna tomorrow instead. It would give him enough time to work out how to season the humble pie he'd be eating.

Gunnar parked in his driveway, frowning as he spotted the cat from next door lounging on the cushion of his patio chair. The last thing he needed was more friction with his neighbor. Hopefully, it wouldn't try to follow him inside.

He got out of his car and unloaded a bag of groceries, keeping an eye on the cat.

The purr of a German engine sounded behind him, and Gunnar turned around as Johanna pulled up in her Audi. Their gazes locked before he could pretend he hadn't seen her.

He might as well eat his crow now rather than delaying his apology until later. He waited for her to park in her detached garage. She'd have to walk past him to get to her front door.

Johanna came out, a purse slung over her arm. She was wearing something different from what she'd had on for their meeting. The calf-length pink dress skimmed her figure, floating around her legs like a ballerina's skirt.

Gunnar hated himself for noticing. He stepped forward, forcing his mouth to form words so his thoughts wouldn't dwell on that dress. "Johanna, do you have a minute?"

She stopped and faced him, raising her chin. "What is it?"

"I owe you an apology for earlier today."

Her eyes widened. "Oh. Okay."

"You were right—I was condescending."

"And rude."

He gritted his teeth. She wasn't making this easy. But he was going to do this apology and do it right, so his conscience could finally shut up. "Yes, I was less than polite. And I'm sorry. That's not how I run my business. You're fully justified in not wanting to work with me, and I respect that decision. But I feel I owe you, at the very least, a proper free half-hour consultation, just like I give all my prospective clients, whether they hire me or not."

There. A perfect apology, served with an offer of free labor. His self-abasement was complete.

Seconds ticked by as she searched his face.

He held her gaze, resisting the impulse to fill the silence with words.

She spoke first. "That's very generous of you, and I accept your apology."

"Thank you." He turned to go into his house. Thank goodness that was over.

"Wait a minute."

He froze. She still wanted to talk?

She gestured with her hands. "It's hard to admit, but you were right about my being unprepared. I didn't know what I didn't know. In fact, I still don't. But you helped me realize where to start, so I think I've already had my free consultation."

He hadn't expected that from her. Crow didn't taste so bad after all. "You're... welcome?"

Her fingers flew to the back of her neck. "The thing is, I really do need a business coach. A... um... friend of mine might be able to connect me to a good sponsorship opportunity, but he wants to see a business plan as soon as possible. I don't know how to make one, and I'd rather not waste time trying to find another consultant. If you're willing to work with someone who's so clueless, I'm happy to give it another try."

She still wanted to hire him. But did he really want to work with her? He shifted his weight to his other foot.

"Um, okay. Complete blank slate. If you give me your email address, I'll send you my terms."

"Sure.   It's johanna@johannastrand.no."

"Nice and easy to remember," he said. "I'll email you right away. If you're happy with the terms, I'm available to talk tomorrow at ten AM."

"Excellent. And this time, I'll bring the information you wanted." Her lips curved into a smile that lit up her brown eyes.

He nodded his goodbye and headed to his front door.

The cat sat up, stretching languidly on the chair. It licked one massive paw, fixing a green-eyed stare on Gunnar. His hand itched to pet it, but that might not be a good idea with Johanna standing right there.

"Cleo! Come here," Johanna called out from behind him.

The cat hopped down and strolled toward her.

Gunnar opened his front door and went inside, shutting the door quickly behind him. He was actually going to work with the cat lady. Good grief.

Chapter 11

OHANNA LET CLEO INTO the house ahead of her and shut the door.

She'd spent a fortune on cat furniture, cat toys, and a fun little exercise run. But Cleo ignored it all and wanted to lie around on Gunnar's patio chair. What was so great about his cushions?

When it came to that, what was in him that her friends and her cat saw, but that she was clearly missing? At least he was willing to own up to his bad behavior and give her a full apology. That moved him up a small notch.

They'd probably never be best friends, but at least they could be civil. And now she'd get the help she needed to put together a business plan to show to Anton.

Her cheek tingled where Anton had kissed it. Those gray eyes looking into hers...

A message came through on her phone. It was Anton. Her heart skittered.

Lunch was wonderful, and you looked sensational. I'm looking forward to hearing how you're going to take on the world. Send me that business plan soonest.

Johanna bit her lip. She should have told Anton she didn't have a business plan to speak of. But then he might have thought less of her.

She typed a reply.

I enjoyed lunch, too. I'm working with a business coach to update my plan now that I'm doing this full time. Looking forward to sharing it with you.

That was just a slight shading of the truth. Her "plan" was a vague collection of thoughts, and she did have a verbal agreement to work with Gunnar. Had he sent that email yet?

She checked the email app on her phone. Gunnar's email was already sitting in her inbox. She skimmed over the text, coming to his hourly rate. She winced. He certainly wasn't charging her a friends' discount. But why should he? They weren't friends.

Her reply to him was brief.

Terms accepted. See you tomorrow.

The next morning, Johanna arrived at Lukas's ranch-style house, which doubled as the office where he and Gunnar worked.

She carried a document file tucked under her arm and stuffed with every piece of data she could imagine about her business. It had taken her half the night to compile all this information, but she wasn't going to come up short again. Gunnar would have no reason to call her unprepared today.

Inger-Britt, the pretty receptionist, greeted her with a pleasant smile. "Mr.

Rikardson is expecting you. Please follow me."

"No need to trouble yourself. I know the way to his office."

"He's not in his office." The young woman stood, showing off the kind of legs Johanna could only have dreamed of twenty years ago. "This way, please."

Johanna followed her into the back-yard and toward the newly built garden cabin. Bethany had mentioned that Lukas was planning on using the small outbuilding for more office space, but Johanna hadn't yet had a chance to check it out since construction had finished. Rather than the rustic design Johanna expected, the cabin was an ultra-modern blend of wood, glass, and metal.

Inger-Britt stood outside the sliding doors. "He's in there. Would you like something to drink?"

"A black coffee would be wonderful, please."

Gunnar came up to the door. "Hi, Johanna. Come in, please. Thanks, Inger-Britt."

Color bloomed on the girl's cheeks as she walked away.

Well, well, well. What was going on there? Johanna recognized that look all too clearly. There must be a good twenty years between Gunnar and that girl. But it wasn't any of her business.

The interior of the cabin was decorated like a comfortable lounge, with deep armchairs and handmade rugs.

Gunnar motioned her toward one of the armchairs.

She held up her folder. "I've got all the information you wanted here. Engagement rates, blog traffic, subscriber numbers—the whole nine yards."

"Thanks." He took the folder from her. "We won't need that just yet. I want to take a different, rather roundabout approach."

"Roundabout?" She didn't like the sound of that. "I was hoping you'd help me make a business plan as soon as possible. I have a friend who might be able to get me sponsors for my YouTube channel, but I have to show him a business plan."

Gunnar nodded, setting the folder on the coffee table between them.

"We'll get there. You just need to trust the process. Please sit down."

Johanna lowered herself onto the armchair. "Will this roundabout process get me a business plan by the end of this week?"

Gunnar started to speak, but stopped as Inger-Britt approached the sliding glass doors with a loaded tray. He got to his feet and pushed the door opening wider, standing aside as the young woman stepped into the room.

She laid the tray on the table. There were two mugs of coffee and bottled water alongside a plate of muffins and brownie fingers.

"Thanks, Inger-Britt," Gunnar said. "That'll be all for now."

Johanna watched Gunnar and his PA with interest. Didn't he notice the doe-eyed, lash-fluttering glances from the blushing girl? The man was either clueless or made of stone. Or a good actor. His expression never changed as he spoke to her, and his gaze didn't follow her perfect figure as she left the cabin.

He settled back into his armchair. "Please help yourself."

"Thanks." Johanna could use that coffee after her late night. It was scalding hot, exactly how she liked it. "Mmm, this is good. So, you don't need all that information I pulled together?" She gestured at the folder which now lay next to his chair.

He shook his head. "Those numbers are just a snapshot of where your business is at the moment. While they're important to know, they don't tell me or you about the direction in which it's going."

Her coffee mug froze partway to her mouth as she stared at him. "Then why did you make such a big deal out of them yesterday?"

He winced, putting his cup down. "Nice gotcha. I often ask my clients for that kind of information on our first meeting, just to gage how serious they are."

"So you can intimidate the tire kickers and scare them away?"

His sudden laugh surprised her.

"No, the intention isn't to intimidate. Asking a client about their business is supposed to build a rapport with them, because people are often comfortable talking about that. But I clearly botched that meeting. Can we just forget about it?"

She smiled back. "What meeting?"

"I have no idea what you're talking about." His eyes twinkled. "Let's get to what you're actually paying me for, which is business consulting."

Johanna nodded, settling back in her chair.

Gunnar mirrored her movement. "For a moment, let's assume that money wasn't a hindrance. Imagine that whatever you chose to do, you could earn a living doing that, but it might mean months of hard work, putting in longer hours than you ever did as a real estate agent. Would you still want to be a social media chef?"

"Absolutely. I loved doing it even before I made a single coin out of it."

"What made you start doing it?" His gaze didn't leave her face.

"A friend of mine who lives in the UK wanted to know how I make my almond cake. Instead of writing up the recipe, I thought it would be fun to film myself cooking. She loved the video and shared it with her family and other friends. Then strangers began commenting on it and asking for more videos."

"Why did you make these videos instead of pointing your friend to an online recipe or cookery show or YouTube channel? That would have been a lot easier. Why do it yourself?"

The questions were getting hard to answer. Johanna took a sip of coffee as she grasped for the correct words. "I don't want to sound arrogant, but I feel like I have a message to share along with my food. And putting it online means that message can reach beyond just the few people I know in real life."

"And what message is that?"

She started to talk, then stopped short. What *was* that message? That it was fun to cook? That they should make their meals from scratch? "I... I don't know. I can't quite put it into words." She looked into his face. "And please don't tell me again that I'm unprepared."

"Figuring out the core message of your business—why you do what you do—is a very challenging exercise. My clients usually have to dig really deep to find their answer. And I don't go forward with helping them with their business plan until they can articulate why their business exists."

"Whoa." She held up her hands. "Isn't it enough to just say the business exists so they can pay some bills or make a living? Why all the soul-searching stuff?"

He laughed again. It was a nice sound. "I understand what you mean." His smile disappeared, and he leaned forward. "Succeeding as a small business is really hard, especially when you're a one-person show. It can be a long slog with little reward for a long time. Unless you have a clear vision of what you're doing and why you're doing it, it's very easy to throw in the towel.

"That's why I encourage people to do something they're passionate about, and to have a strong reason why they're doing it. And it can't just be because they want money. There are many other ways of making money. In fact, they're probably much easier than what you're trying to do."

"You're full of encouragement," Johanna said.

"Well, if running a successful small business was easy, everyone would be doing it, right? You're already ahead of most because you were doing this social media chef thing just for fun. Meaning that you enjoy it, and maybe even have a passion for it. So, I want us to uncover the kernel of that passion, that undying ember that will keep you fired up even when the going gets tough. Because things will get tough."

Johanna let his words sink in. He didn't sound at all like all those "Rah rah, quick success, make money while you sleep" types she'd found on her quick internet search for business coaches.

She said, "So my vision will help keep me motivated."

"Yes. And there's another crucial reason why need to nail your vision. It'll keep you focused and make important decisions easier. Like, should you make this or that type of content? Should you accept a sponsor? Should you partner up with another influencer? Should you give up trying to make a business out of this and just keep it as a hobby?"

Johanna bristled at his last words.

Gunnar held up his hand. He must have read something in her face. "I'm not trying to disrespect your abilities. I'm just saying you have to be completely honest with yourself and ask yourself the hard questions. Even when the answers aren't what you want to hear. Sometimes, it might be that you're not even supposed to be making a business out of this particular thing."

"So, are you telling me you've had clients whom you've actually talked out of their business idea? Doesn't that mean you've talked yourself out of a job?"

"Yes, it's happened a few times. But it's not about me talking them out of their business idea. I just guided them through the process of figuring out their vision. They realized for themselves that they're better off doing something else. Either a different business or maybe not a business at all."

Johanna stared at him. He was definitely not one of those "overnight success" gurus.

Gunnar said, "I have a process I'll take you through, and it's up to you to have the courage to answer those questions honestly, wherever they lead. Even if it leads you to conclude that going full time isn't right for you. Or that you can't go full time within the time frame that you wanted. And since I know you're a Christian, I hope you'll go through this process prayerfully, asking for God's guidance and discernment."

Johanna took a deep breath and let it out slowly. She wasn't expecting things to get this intense. "Well, I already know that you won't spare my feelings when it comes to telling the truth."

"I'll try to season my words with grace going forward, but, yes, I don't believe in lying to my clients. It doesn't help anyone."

"What if I'm scared about the answers I'll find? What if I go through this process of yours and it turns out that I don't have a viable business at all?"

"Oh, I think your business is viable, on paper at least, based on what I've seen other people do. I spent a few hours last night binge-watching your videos. They're highly entertaining, and I could tell you had fun making them."

A flush of pleasure swelled inside her chest. Somehow, that compliment meant a lot coming from him.

He leaned forward. "I'm not here to tell you what to do. This is about you and your decisions. So, are you ready to get to work?"

Chapter 12

UNNAR CROSSED THE YARD and headed for the cabin office. Johanna had been working for an hour, and it was time to check on her progress.

Their talk earlier that morning had gone surprisingly well, and he was looking forward to hearing what she'd come up with.

She'd abandoned her armchair and sat cross-legged on the floor, balancing a notebook on her knee. Several sheets of loose paper lay strewn around her.

As he walked into the room, she looked up at him. "Don't mind the mess. I think I'm done."

"Already? My clients usually need a few days or even weeks to do their vision work." He lowered himself onto the floor opposite her. "So, have you come to the heart of why you want to be a social media chef?"

"Yes. Although…" She chewed the end of her pen, her face flushing. "I'm not sure I've got the phrasing right, but I know what I want to say."

"I wasn't expecting perfection."

"Good, because this is very rough." She looked at her notes. "Most of my closest friends are single, or at least they have been single until fairly recently. And among singles, I've noticed that eating alone at home often has a rather pathetic ring to it. It feels like you're eating alone because you don't have someone to share a meal with, and you're having that lonely meal at home because you can't afford to eat out. But I don't think it has to be like that. Why can't meals for one at home feel like a celebration, or a self-care treat?"

Why not, indeed? Gunnar's mind went to the stack of frozen dinners in his own freezer. Eating was just something he did to fuel his body and move on to the next thing. He often ate standing up at his kitchen counter. There was little joy or celebration in it, and there didn't seem to be much point in putting in extra effort when the meal was just for him. "So, you want to help people make meals for one special?"

"Yes." Her face lit up as she spoke. "There's a lot of content about making meals for families or for parties or romantic meals for two. I haven't seen much out there for people who are making a meal just for themselves. And yet why shouldn't a person have a delicious dinner for one? Why can't you take the trouble to make a nice dinner for yourself just because you're special enough?"

Color flooded Johanna's cheeks. "I mean, of course, the general you. Not specifically you, as in Gunnar."

"No, I get your meaning." She was surprisingly cute when she was flustered and embarrassed. But he wasn't supposed to notice things like that. "I think it would resonate with a lot of people. A meal for one can be a celebration or a treat."

"That's it. I mean, people often make meals for four and split them into single portions. But I want to focus on specific meals for one. You think that sounds like a good 'why'?"

Gunnar nodded. "Absolutely. You're excited about it and it's easy to explain. And you've also gone one step further and covered my next question, because this is something around which you can create a lot of content."

"Yay! I'm so thrilled about it." Her face glowed. "I wasn't sure I was on the right track."

Her excitement was infectious. "I think you're on to something that has a lot of potential. Have you thought about what you could do beyond YouTube?"

Johanna frowned. "What do you mean, 'beyond YouTube'?"

"This is beyond the scope of today's session and should go into your business plan, but I think you should consider offering paid content, like a membership platform or online courses. YouTube monetization is a great start, but I think you could do a lot more to secure a more stable income."

Her eyes widened. "I hadn't thought about that at all. You really think people might want to pay for my content?"

"That's a topic for another day but, in short, yes. I think we should end today's consultation here, though.

You've covered a lot of ground. Are you ready for some homework?"

"Yes." She held her pen poised over a fresh page in her notebook.

"Your newly defined niche is meals for one. In preparation for our next session, I want you to audit all the content you've already made that fits within this niche. All the videos, the blog posts, the Instagram posts. Check out how your audience responded to it. If the content fell flat, don't worry too much. It could mean that your current audience may not want to go in that direction and you'll need to build a whole new audience."

"Gotcha," she said, scribbling in her notebook. She looked back at him. "Thanks so much. I don't remember the last time I felt so energized about my business."

He knew the feeling. "You're welcome. Take a good rest and I'll see you next time."

Chapter 13

JOHANNA RAN HER GAZE down her voice-over script one final time. Sitting in her recording booth at home, she still felt the buzz of excitement after yesterday's session with Gunnar. It was going to be so much fun to concentrate on meals for one.

She should rebrand her content channels and give them a different name that went along with her niche. "Meals for One" was the obvious name, but a bit of a cliché. What about "Eating Solo?" Or perhaps "Table for

One." She liked that. "A Solitary Feast?" No, that sounded too much like binge eating. "Dining Alone" might work, too. And maybe she should hire a videographer to give her videos a bit more of a professional polish.

Lukas had been spot on—Gunnar was a stellar coach. Within just a couple of hours, he'd helped her align her interests with a promising niche and made her feel as though anything was possible.

Going to bed had been a challenge with her mind a whirl of ideas for new recipes and videos to record, and although it was Saturday, she'd risen well before seven to try out a few things. Now, she was ready to start her first new cooking video, or at least the voice-over audio that would go with it.

Johanna hit the red button on her recording software and spoke into her microphone. "In my hunt for the perfect soufflé, I've gone through ten different recipes so you don't have to. You're welcome. I've tried sweet and—" She turned her head. What was that banging noise?

Although the little booth converted from her hallway closet was well sound-proofed and shut out most noises, her microphone could still pick up sounds like lawn mowers and sirens. Or the muffled rhythmical thuds that were coming from somewhere outside.

She waited a few seconds until the noises died down, then resumed recording. "In my hunt for the perfect homemade soufflé, I've gone through ten different—are you serious?"

She clicked off the recording software and stepped out into the hallway. What was that noise? If she found where it was coming from, she could gage whether it was likely to stop soon, or if it was a persistent activity that she needed either to wait out or deal with.

The sounds became louder as she walked toward her back door. It was coming from next door. From Gunnar's place.

The reason for the noise became all too clear as she stepped outside onto her patio. Gunnar, Lukas, and Lukas's brother Kai were outside the house, all dressed in work clothes. Kai was on his hands and knees, hammering a wooden plank into place. Today of all days, when she wanted to do voice-over work for a couple of videos, they were building a deck. There was no way she could carry on with that racket, and she couldn't ask them to stop. She'd just have to do something else until they were done.

She turned to go back inside and paused as a shout floated over the air.

"Hi, Johanna. What's up?"

Great. Now she'd have to make small talk. She faced Lukas, stretching her lips into a smile. "Hi. You're looking busy."

"We had to help this city boy." Lukas put an arm around Gunnar's shoulders.

"Hey," Gunnar said, "I resent the implication that being from the city means I can't do DIY."

Lukas leaned forward, staring pointedly at his friend's left thumb, which was swathed in a bandage.

Gunnar whipped his hand behind his back, prompting chuckles from his friends.

Johanna covered her mouth to hide her smile. "I'll leave you to it."

She caught a flash of movement in the corner of her eye. Looking toward where it came from, her gaze landed on Cleo. The cat lay sunning herself on the grass next to the construction area. The feline had no problem with the loud noises that came with building Gunnar's deck, and yet she would bolt and hide whenever Johanna turned on the food processor.

"Cats are crazy," Johanna muttered.

Since recording was out of the question, she'd get on with work that didn't require silence. Like some of that homework Gunnar wanted her to do before their next session on Monday.

She retrieved her laptop from the recording booth and carried it to her desk. Where were her notes from her consultation session?

She pulled out her notebook and flipped through to what she'd written yesterday. Gunnar wanted her to check her existing videos, blog and social media posts for content that fit the "Table for One" theme and to note how her audience had responded to them.

She opened her YouTube channel. With over seven hundred videos uploaded over the years, this homework was going to take a while. She started with her oldest videos, working her way through in chronological order.

Her phone rang and she glanced at her watch. How had three hours gone by? She crossed the room and picked up the phone, her heart fluttering when she saw the caller ID.

"Hi, Anton."

"Hey. I thought I was going to see a business plan from you after our lunch."

Johanna squirmed. She hadn't expected him to follow up this soon. And now he'd think she was a slacker.

"To be honest, I haven't had a proper plan beyond some ideas in my head. But I've started working with a business coach to put the plan together, and I'm very excited about what we've done so far. He's helped me pin down a focus niche."

"Oh? What niche is that?"

"I'm thinking of calling my channel Table for One. It'll be all about making solo dining at home fun and something to look forward to instead of to dread and avoid. I've got loads of recipes and hacks to share."

Anton was silent for so long that Johanna wondered whether the call had dropped.

She glanced at her handset. "Hello?"

"Oh, yeah, no, I'm here. Table for One." His tone was flat. "Who did you say your business coach is? Where did you find him?"

"A friend recommended him. He's had some really good results with other clients."

"Right. And is he the one who suggested this idea?"

Johanna's enthusiasm faltered. Didn't Anton like the concept? "No, it was my idea. I think it has a lot of potential beyond just attracting sponsors. I was doing some research around creating a paid membership community and I'm really excited about the possibilities."

"I see. Well, if he's a good coach and not out to make a fast buck by giving you false hopes, he should know that it's probably best not to run before you can walk. Linking your brand to a corporate sponsor is where I think you should focus right now."

A chill swept over Johanna. Anton hadn't exactly popped her bubble, but his underwhelming reaction had put a slow puncture in her excitement. "Okay."

"I can't say too much right now, but my father is very interested in doing what he can to help. I might have some news for you next week."

"Wow, really?" She perked up.

"I'll be in touch."

He ended the call just as a knock sounded on the door.

Johanna went to answer it.

Gunnar stood on her porch, holding Cleo in his arms. "The guys and I are about to eat and I'm sure you wouldn't want her begging for people food or, even worse, getting it."

She took the cat from him, sinking her cheek into Cleo's warm flank. "Thanks."

He turned to leave, then wavered. "You're welcome to join us if you like. We're just grilling a few burgers. Bethany and Lisa are stopping by, too."

His invitation caught her off-guard. Her friends Bethany and Lisa were married to Gunnar's deck-building helpers. It would be nice to hang out with them, and her empty stomach reminded her it had been ages since she ate. But she had work to do. When Anton called next week, she wanted to be fully on top of everything.

She shook her head. "It's nice of you to ask, but I've got other plans. Thanks."

As she closed the door behind him, she half-regretted her answer. But there was no other option.

Chapter 14

GUNNAR'S EMAIL CAME THROUGH as Johanna saved her updated spreadsheet. She was almost done after hours of work throughout the weekend, broken only by the time she spent in church. She was stoked about their session later today.

He must be an early bird like she was. How else could he be sending emails at six o'clock on a Monday morning? He probably had some more instructions or information about what they were going to do.

Frowning, she read the message.

I'm very sorry about the late notice but, due to a family emergency, I have to travel out of town and must cancel today's appointment.

I'll be in touch to reschedule as soon as I can. Apologies once again.

Kind regards,

Gunnar.

What kind of emergency was it? It sounded serious. She knew nothing about Gunnar's family. He'd moved here from Trondheim, and his dialect indicated that he'd grown up in that part of Norway. Presumably that's where his family was. Had someone died?

She read through the email again, searching for clues between the sparse lines, then bowed her head.

Lord, please be with Gunnar's family. You know what they need, and I ask that you provide them with it.

She clicked the reply button, hesitating for a few seconds before typing.

No problem. Praying that all will go well.

That last sentence was dumb. What if someone had died? She deleted the words and typed again.

Thanks for letting me know. Praying for the family.

She hit "send." Whatever was going on must be really urgent if he needed to drop everything and go. It would be inappropriate to press him for details, but maybe she could ask Bethany later for an update.

In the meantime, she had an unexpectedly free day on her hands. She shouldn't waste it, although she was disappointed about her canceled session with Gunnar.

The homework he'd asked her to do was done. Since there wouldn't be any more carpentry noise from next door, she could finish her voice-overs. And when that was done, she needed to look into hiring a videographer to give her content more of a professional polish.

She flipped her daily planner open and crossed out her appointment with Gunnar, then penciled in a new to-do list.

By eight o'clock, she was done with the voice-overs and ready to move on to the next item on her list.

Her phone rang. Anton? "Hey, good morning."

"Morning, Johanna. I hope I'm not calling too early, but I hoped to catch you before you get busy today. Do you have any plans for lunch?"

"No, I'm actually free today."

"Good. My father wants to speak with you about a proposal I think you might find interesting. Can you meet us at the country club at one o'clock?"

Johanna's stomach backflipped like an Olympic gymnast. "Yes, I can do that."

"Great. Wear something nice. See you soon."

Johanna put the phone down. What did Anton consider nice? He'd complimented the dress she wore last time, so she should choose something similar.

Her hand went up to her short hair. Could her hairdresser squeeze her in for a shampoo and blow dry?

She jumped up and grabbed her purse, ignoring Cleo's reproachful stare.

Gunnar stroked his mother's fingers, his heart shattering into a million pieces. Her hand felt so fragile he was afraid he might crush it, and her pretty pastel house coat didn't hide how waif thin she was.

He couldn't bring himself to look at the walker that stood next to her bed. She'd not needed one before. How had she gone downhill so fast since the last time he'd seen her? A painful lump swelled in the back of his throat.

The warm, strong light in her eyes was the same as always, though. "I'm so happy to see you, Gunnar. I know how busy you are, so it's such a wonderful surprise. Berghaven is so far away."

"I came as soon as Pappa told me about your fall. How are you feeling? Should you be out of the hospital?"

"I'm not too bad, considering." She raised her other hand, which was freshly encased in a cast. "The doctor said it could have been a lot worse. And since it's just a wrist fracture, they agreed I'd be more comfortable at home."

Pappa's gravely voice came from behind Gunnar. "With the fall she had, she could have broken her hip or had a head injury. It was just by God's grace that all she had was a broken wrist."

Mamma squeezed Gunnar's hand. "Enough about me and my boring ailments. Tell me what you're up to up north. How's work getting on? Are you making friends? I worry about you being alone and so far away."

"Work is going well, and I've met some very nice people. You know Lukas, of course, and I've also come to know his wife and their friends. And I've found a lovely church."

"That's wonderful. Your father showed me that picture you sent from your front yard. It's so strange that there aren't any trees up there."

He made small talk about his life in Berghaven, describing the town and surrounding countryside. Mamma drank in every detail. Gunnar's voice faltered when it hit him that she'd probably never see the town where he now lived.

Throughout their conversation, they skirted around the elephant in the room—his relationship with his brother. He wasn't sure who was avoiding the topic: he because he was ashamed, or Mamma because she didn't want him to feel bad. But the words hung unspoken between them. A fractured family, broken thanks to his actions.

Too soon, Pappa touched his shoulder. "Let's let your mother get some rest now."

Mamma protested, but Gunnar stood. It was time to go. The longer he stayed, the greater the chances he would run into Stefan. His brother would definitely show up to check on Mamma. And if Stefan saw him, it might cause an ugly scene. He couldn't put Mamma through that. His visit with her, though cruelly short, was running out.

He reached out, circling her with his arms as though she were made of glass. All his life, her hugs had been the ones to give him comfort and strength. Now, he was afraid he'd snap her in half.

As though reading his mind, she said, "Give me a proper hug, darling. I won't break."

He pulled her closer, blinking away tears. "I'll call when I'm back in Berghaven."

She didn't ask why he was leaving town so soon, and the fact that she didn't question his going ripped into his heart.

Pappa followed him out to the hallway. "She really should be getting morphine, but she doesn't want it."

"Is she in a lot of pain?"

"All the time. But she doesn't let it show."

They stood in silence for a moment, then Pappa said, "It would mean the world to her if you and Stefan could both be at our anniversary party."

Gunnar's gaze dropped to the floor. "I know."

"Is there any way you could make it right?"

Gunnar forced himself to look his father in the face. Pappa's eyes carried the same wistful yearning he'd read in Mamma's. "I'd do anything to reverse time, or undo my mistakes. But Stefan is the one I wronged, so I think it's only fair that he gets to decide when he's ready to let bygones be bygones."

"Okay." Pappa's shoulders slumped. He said something about the weather, and Gunnar was relieved to talk about the likelihood of a heatwave this summer.

Pappa never brought up the rift between his sons, and for him to speak of it now told of how keenly he wanted some show of reconciliation for his wife's sake.

Gunnar glanced at his watch. He was running a big risk staying so long. Stefan might show up at any minute. He'd better head for the airport to catch his flight back home.

It was strange that when he thought of home now, the place that came to his mind wasn't Trondheim, the city where he'd been born and lived all his life, but Berghaven. The town where he'd exiled himself, where his closest friends lived, and where his house was next to an infuriating neighbor with an imperious cat. It would be good to return home.

Chapter 15

JOHANNA'S HEART HAMMERED AS Anton's gaze swept over her. She'd chosen a flowery blouse with lantern sleeves paired with a calf-length mermaid skirt.

He held out his arm. "You look stunning."

She slipped her hand into the crook of his elbow and let him steer her toward the dining room of the Havdal Country Club.

"My father's already seated. He's been looking forward to seeing you."

Einar Einarson stood as Johanna approached with his son. The older businessman gave a glimpse of what Anton might look like in thirty years. His hair, the color of a snow-sprinkled mountain, was still thick and freshly barbered. His expensive suit fitted him impeccably.

He greeted her with a kiss on the cheek. "Thank you so much for making the time to meet us. Please sit down. Has Anton told you much?"

Johanna shook her head as she settled into the padded chair.

Anton sat next to her and inclined his head toward his father. "I thought it best to let you share the news."

"No, you go ahead. You know the vocabulary."

Johanna gripped the edge of her seat. Would either of them finally tell her what this news was?

Anton smiled, turning to Johanna. "Remember when I told you that we knew some people who might be open to sponsor your content if it matched their brand?"

"Yes," Johanna said, working to keep her voice level.

"One of my father's associates owns a pet supplement company. You may have heard of them. They're called Nutrivite."

"I've heard of them. They make mail order vitamins and herbal supplements for pets."

Beaming, Mr. Einarson pointed at Johanna and spoke to his son. "See? What did I tell you? She's on the ball."

Her cheeks warmed at his compliment.

Anton leaned forward. "Marit Furuvik owns Nutrivite, and she's especially keen on working with other women entrepreneurs. I showed her your YouTube channel, and she immediately homed in on the video where you made snacks for your cat. Remember that one?"

Johanna did. She'd thought it would be fun to make a video about creating homemade treats for Cleo just in case someone else felt like spoiling their cat. "Sure, that was a fun one to make."

"Nutrivite wants to sponsor your channel. They'll pay you to mention their products and are especially interested in you creating pet recipes that include their supplements. They like your overall YouTube subscriber numbers, but they'd like a breakdown on how many views you get on your pet-related videos. They're ready to negotiate terms and conditions. And, just as an aside, I think it would be a good idea for you to upload a few more pet food related videos over the next couple of days. So, what do you think?"

Anton and Mr. Einarson looked at her expectantly.

Heat rushed to her face. "That's really huge news."

"I thought you'd be pleased." Anton grinned. "I know something of what they pay some of their other content creators, especially if you come up with a creative way to highlight their brand."

Johanna smiled back. Homemade cat snacks? She had maybe two or three videos with cat food recipes, although Cleo appeared in several of her uploads, just looking pretty for the camera. Making content about pet treats would be a significant shift in focus from what she'd been doing up to now. And what about the "Table for One" idea? Could she build both brands? Just one niche was going to take up all her time and energy. How was she going to manage two?

"I told Marit what a hardworking young lady you are and that I have no hesitation in vouching for you," Mr. Einarson said. "If you contact my secretary, she'll put you in touch with Marit, and you can take it from there."

"I appreciate that," Johanna said. "It sounds like a great opportunity."

Mr. Einarson leaned back in his seat. "I don't often do this sort of thing for people because I've been burned in the past when putting someone's name forward. You tie your reputation to a person's when you recommend them for a thing like this. But Anton and I are sure that you can make it work."

Johanna didn't know what to answer to that. "I'm very humbled by your confidence in me."

"It's well justified, and it's the least I could do, especially since Anton led me to understand that we indirectly led to your parting ways with your former employer."

Johanna shook her head. "Please don't feel responsible for that. It was a long time coming and would have happened sooner or later."

"All the same, I'm very glad to help." He lifted up his glass. "Here's to your bright new future. What, you don't have a drink? Anton, please call the waiter."

As Anton waved down the waiter, Johanna tried to wrap her mind around everything he and his father had said.

"Sparkling water with lemon, please," she said to the waiter.

Mr. Einarson sipped from his own glass. "And when you've brought everyone's drinks, we'll be ready for our lunch." He turned to Johanna. "I recommend the char-grilled Caesar salad. But you're the food expert. I should listen to what you recommend."

Johanna smiled back, her mind still focused on this new idea. Although she was confident enough to have a channel for people food, she was no expert on cat nutrition. Her cat treats were something she just did for fun, and weren't meant to replace Cleo's regular meals. How would she create enough cat food recipes to fill an entire channel? What if someone held her liable because their pet got sick?

But Mr. Einarson and Anton's willingness to vouch for her warmed her to her core. She didn't want to let them down.

Perhaps she wouldn't do full pet meals, then. Cat snacks might be enough. The occasional delicious treat for one's cat on top of its regular meals. That sounded far more workable, and she could still make fun videos about that.

When she next met with Gunnar, she'd explain to him that she was exploring a new direction. This opportunity was too good to pass up without giving it a chance.

The waiter returned to the table with a tray of drinks. He placed a glass of sparkling water in front of Johanna and some sort of green cocktail for Anton.

Mr. Einarson raised his glass. "To a bright and successful future. I expect great things from you, Johanna. *Skål.*"

She lifted her glass. "*Skål.*"

Her gaze met Anton's, and he winked at her.

After lunch, Anton walked Johanna to her car.

He turned toward her as she stood next to her door. "I've got a great feeling about Nutrivite. I don't know whether you understand what a big deal it is, first of all to get an opportunity like that, and second, for my father to be willing to put your name forward. His name means everything to him."

"I'll do my best."

"I know you will. There's one more thing." He gave her a crooked smile.

"I'm running out of business-related excuses to see you. Would you mind if I asked you out just because?"

Her heart fluttered. "No, I wouldn't mind that at all."

"Do you have any plans for this weekend?"

He wanted to see her that soon? She did her best to keep her cool. "Actually, I do. I'm having my friends over for a barbecue on Saturday. If you're free, you're more than welcome."

He folded his arms and stroked his chin with one thumb. "I was thinking more along the lines of having you to myself. But, sure, a barbecue sounds good. What time?"

"One o'clock?"

"Okay. See you then."

He leaned forward, and her heart seized up. Was he going to kiss her? His lips grazed her hairline, and he stood back. He gave her a wave, then headed back to the clubhouse.

Chapter 16

JOHANNA GOT COMFORTABLE ON her patio later that evening. Her laptop was on the table in front of her, but she did her best thinking with pen and paper. And she had a lot of thinking to do.

It had taken all afternoon, a clothes shopping spree, and the forty-five minute drive from Havdal for her mind to simmer down from the excitement of Anton wanting to date.

Now, perhaps she could gather her wits together and think about her business. She was supposed to contact

Mr. Einarson's secretary about getting in touch with Nutrivite, but she wanted to prepare herself first. It would be terrible if she came across as unprepared, like in her first meeting with Gunnar.

She turned over a fresh page in her notebook and wrote, "Feline Dining." That had a nice ring to it. Or maybe she shouldn't use the word "dining" at all since that implied meals and she was just making treats.

She ought to start by researching Nutrivite and the supplements it made, then think about how to incorporate them into her homemade cat food recipes. Then she could make something for Cleo and film a reaction video.

There was so much work to do.

She opened up her laptop to look up Nutrivite, then lifted her head up at the sound of a car pulling into Gunnar's driveway. Was he back already?

Yes, it was him. Gunnar climbed slowly out of his late model Volkswagen SUV, showing a flash of mismatched socks in his brown leather loafers. She glanced at his face. His eyes were red-rimmed. He caught her gaze before she had the sense to stop staring.

There was nothing for it. She'd have to say hi.

She got up and walked to the edge of her patio. "You're back in town? I thought you left this morning."

What a dumb question. Of course he was back in town.

He nodded, shouldering a gray backpack. "I was able to catch an evening flight back from Trondheim and didn't have to stay the night."

"Is everything okay? I don't mean to pry, but you said you had a family emergency."

"My mother is dying." The words burst out of his mouth.

She took several quick steps toward him. "Oh no, Gunnar, I'm so sorry. Is she sick?"

He angled his body away from her, pressing the heels of his palms against his eyes.

She stopped a couple of feet away from him, her hands itching to do something. Anything was better than watching him crumble.

He took a long, shuddering breath. "Cancer. She had it some years ago. It seemed to be in remission, but it's back, and the doctors don't think she can beat it this time. We're just waiting."

Her heart ached for him. "How long?"

"Maybe two months, perhaps as long as six. She's at peace with it. Her faith is solid, and she's looking forward to going home." His eyes glistened. "She wants to use the time that's left to make memories and enjoy her family."

"So, the emergency—did she take a turn for the worse? Is that why you went to Trondheim?"

"She fell. She needs a walker now, and I think it was just out of reach.

She blacked out and my father called me when they were running tests. They didn't know how badly she might have been hurt, and I—" his voice cracked. "I just had to see her. When I got there, she was a lot better. She'd broken her wrist in two places, but at least there were no other fractures or a head injury."

"Oh, no. Is she in pain?"

"I think they've got that managed, although my father says she doesn't like to take her meds."

His shoulders sagged as he spoke, and it suddenly hit her how exhausted he must be. She had no words of wisdom or comfort to ease his burden, but she did have one thing. Food.

She pointed back toward her house. "I've got some soup and rolls I was planning to heat up for dinner. I don't know whether you've had a chance to eat, but it'll just take me a couple of minutes to get everything ready. We could sit out here on my patio."

For a couple of seconds, she thought he was going to say no, and she regretted asking.

Then the lines of his face relaxed, his lips tilting in a smile. "Thank you. I haven't eaten all day."

"Okay, take a seat. I won't be long." She grabbed her laptop and notebooks off the glass-topped patio table and went inside.

In her kitchen, she tipped a container of homemade leek and potato soup into a pot and set it on the stovetop, then dug out a bag of frozen din-

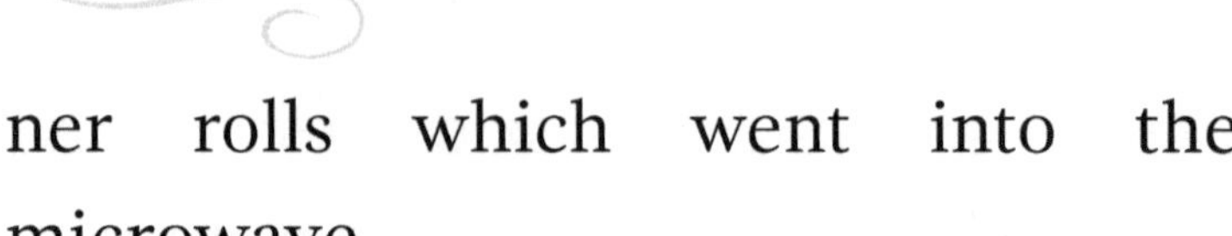

ner rolls which went into the microwave.

When everything was heated up, she carried the tray out to the patio.

Gunnar sat leaning back in a garden chair, with Cleo curled up on his lap. He straightened up. "Sorry, she just hopped up, and I didn't have the heart to put her down."

Johanna put the tray on the table. "If you're happy and she's happy, then I'm happy. No need to move her." Why had she ever been so worked up about Cleo wanting to hang out with Gunnar? It seemed like a lifetime ago. And he looked like he could use a Cleo cuddle.

She passed him a bowl of steaming hot soup and the basket of rolls.

He closed his eyes and bowed his head, then picked up a spoon. His eyebrows flew up as he took his first mouthful of soup. "This is exceptional."

His compliment warmed her. "Thanks. Eat up—I have plenty more."

They ate in silence for a while, the patio bathed in bright summer sunshine even though it was approaching nine o'clock.

This was a picture she could never have predicted a few months ago—she and Gunnar sitting on her patio sharing a meal, with Cleo looking like she owned his lap.

Gunnar's spoon clattered into his empty bowl. He pushed his chair back and stroked Cleo's fur. "That was beyond delicious. Thank you. My mother used to make that soup, except she would put bacon bits on top. She loved to cook."

Johanna hesitated before stepping out onto uncharted waters. The last thing she wanted to do was to cause him more pain. "Do you want to talk about her?"

He looked up at her, his eyes widening. "Actually, yes. I'd like that."

She exhaled slowly, relieved that he hadn't taken offense. "What was she like when you were growing up?"

"She was the most insanely fun person ever. We'd build forts in the living room with blankets and cardboard boxes and pretend we were Vikings coming to sack the town. We had some epic pillow fights." He chuckled. "Once when we were playing, someone rang the doorbell. Mamma was in full barbarian face paint and the living room was a total mess. When she went to the door, she found a group of ladies from church. She'd forgotten that they were coming for coffee. Did I mention she was the pastor's wife?"

Johanna laughed. "No way! She sounds like the coolest mom and pastor's wife ever. What did she do?"

"She just rolled with it. She invited them in and we cleared space on the chairs. My brother and sister and I went off to play in another room, but we heard them all laughing over their coffee, so I think they had a decent time. She could get right down and play with us, but she was strict when she needed to be. We knew which parent we could never cross."

"Did she work outside the home?"

He shook his head. "Not while we were little. When we went to school, I think she started doing some work. She was a trained nurse and did shifts at the local care home. Looking back, I can't imagine how she balanced it all. Work, taking care of us, running the women's and children's ministries at church. She made it look easy."

"Some women do," Johanna said.

He looked up at her. "How about your mother? What's she like?"

"She did her best with what she had. She died a few years ago."

"I'm really sorry. How did she—?"

Johanna winced. "Cancer."

"Oh." His voice was quieter when he spoke again. "It stinks, doesn't it?"

"It does. I'm not going to lie—you're probably in for some really rough times. I'm so glad your mom has her faith. She has the right idea to make the most of the time that's left and enjoy her family. I wish my mother had done that."

"She didn't?"

Johanna shook her head. "She spent her last couple of years running after every crackpot who called themselves a faith healer or snake oil salesman who was hawking an alternative or experimental treatment. I really shouldn't blame her—she was desperate for a cure."

"I can't say I wouldn't have done the same thing."

"Nor me. When she finally agreed to move to the hospice, it was a bit like the woman who touched Jesus's garment. She'd exhausted everything in the hope of a cure. She didn't get healed, obviously, but she found something much better. She recommitted her life to the Lord, and when the end finally came, she was truly at peace." Johanna brushed a tear away from the corner of her eye. "I was supposed to be encouraging you, and now look what I'm doing. I'm making myself cry."

"You are encouraging me," Gunnar said. "I know Mamma will be fine. I'm most worried about how the rest of us will manage when she's gone."

They were quiet for a moment, and his hand moved across Cleo's fur.

Johanna spoke softly. "At first, you'll think you can't make it through that first hour. But you will. Then you'll wonder how you can get to the end of the day. And you'll make it through that. You'll eventually learn how to live with the pain, although it will never completely go away. And we do have the hope of that final re-union. That's the biggest comfort of all. In the meantime, make the most of the time you've got left. Is there any-thing she really, really wants that you can do for her or get for her?"

Gunnar shot her a sharp look, then turned away. It was a long moment be-fore he answered. "There's something she wants very much. I'm doing my best to make it happen, but it's not completely up to me."

She thought he was going to say something else, but he remained silent, his face turned aside.

Then he lifted Cleo off his lap and deposited the big cat onto the patio floor. "Thanks so much for dinner and everything. I'd better get some rest."

He stood, picking up his backpack, and she got to her feet, too. "You're welcome. I'll be praying for your mother and all of you."

"Thanks. I'll need to check with my calendar, but could we reschedule our next session on Wednesday?"

"Sure, that'll be good for me." For a while, she'd forgotten Gunnar was her business coach. He'd felt more like a friend.

He waved. "Good night."

She watched him cross her yard and go into his house.

Chapter 17

GUNNAR THREW HIMSELF ONTO his sòfa. He'd pulled into his driveway, feeling wrung out and exhausted. The last thing he'd expected was a cozy chat with Johanna over a bowl of soup.

He'd told her things not even Lukas knew. And Lukas had definitely never seen him cry about anything. Those few minutes with her had relieved the unbearable pressure that had been building up inside of him all day. He hoped this wouldn't make things awk-ward. He and Johanna still had to work together. And yet he didn't regret talking to her. He sensed that she understood.

His phone rang. It was his sister, Maria. She poured out a flood of words as soon as he hit the green button.

"Gunnar? Finally! I've been trying to get a hold of you for hours. When I went home, Pappa said I'd just missed you and you were flying back north. And all my calls were just going to voice mail."

"I switched my phone off."

"What? Why? And didn't you see my messages when you turned it back on?"

"I did. Sorry." He kneaded the corded muscles between his shoulder and his neck. "Today has been a lot. I didn't know how unwell Mamma is now."

"Oh." Maria's tone softened. "I forgot you haven't seen her since... when was it? Christmas? No, it was January."

"Yeah." He couldn't see Mamma at Christmas because he'd exiled himself from any family gathering where Stefan was expected. "Pappa asked me whether I'll make it for the anniversary party."

"Will you?"

Gunnar sighed. "I was planning on calling you to talk about that, but didn't want to do it today. I think Stefan has blocked my number."

"No. Really? How do you know?"

"When I call him from any of my numbers—private or work—it goes straight to voice mail."

"Did you try his work number?"

"I tried the one I got off LinkedIn and had the same result. But when my office assistant used her personal cellphone, it went straight through. So, I'm pretty sure he's blocked me."

"That doesn't sound good," Maria said. "Do you want me to try to talk to him?"

Her offer dangled in front of him like low-hanging fruit. He could get to know once and for all where he stood with Stefan while using Maria as a shield. But, no. This was something he needed to do for himself. Taking responsibility for his mistakes meant facing the fallout without his sister to soften the blow.

He pushed a hand through his hair. "Thanks, but I'd better keep trying to reach him. I created this problem and I don't want you caught in the middle. If I have to camp out on his doorstep to get a chance to speak to him, that's just how it is."

"You know, I saw her the other day."

Maria's words threw a glacial chill over Gunnar's heart. He didn't have to ask whom she was talking about. "I don't want to know anything about her. Ever."

"Sorry." The unspoken words clanged in the silence.

Finally, Gunnar asked, "How are things going with the preparations for the party?"

"Great. Almost all the RSVPs are in, and a surprising number of guests are going to make it, despite the short notice."

"Glad to hear that." Most of his parents' friends probably knew this might be his mother's last anniversary. Everyone who cared about her would make an effort to be there.

"I have to go now," Maria said. "Keep me posted about what happens with Stefan."

"I will. And please don't try to speak to him on my behalf. I need to sort out my own mess."

"I won't. Bye."

When Maria ended the call, Gunnar went to his computer. He hadn't wanted to use an email to reach out to Stefan, but he didn't have many options left. He'd just have to try. And if he didn't get an answer, he'd try something else. Maybe even show up on Stefan's doorstep.

He opened a new email draft and started to write.

I know you might not want to hear from me, and I fully understand why. I'm deeply sorry for hurting you. What I did to you was unforgivable, and I regret it every day.

I hate putting the burden of this decision on you because you don't deserve it. But I have to ask.

This coming anniversary might be Mamma's last, and it would mean the world for her and Pappa to have all their children at their party. But I also know that it might be painful for you to have me there.

If you feel it's completely unacceptable, I'll stay away. But if you find it possible, could you put aside my offense just for one day, so

Mamma and Pappa can have the celebration they want?

I look forward to your reply.

Before he could change his mind, he hit the "send" button.

Chapter 18

ESPITE WORKING DEEP INTO the previous night, Johanna skipped her usual cup of morning coffee. She was too energized about her meeting with Gunnar to need a caffeine boost. It would be so satisfying to present him with all the progress she'd made since their last business session.

Her negotiations with Nutrivite were going well. The pet supplement company was offering a generous fee to sponsor ten YouTube videos featuring cat treats that included their products. If her audience responded well, they would offer more backing.

Surely, even Gunnar couldn't help but be impressed.

He welcomed her into his office, looking fresh in a crisp blue shirt with folded up sleeves, a far cry from the exhausted man who'd sat on her patio the other night. His blue eyes lit up as she walked toward him, sparking a rush of warmth inside her.

"How's your mother doing?" she asked.

"She's hanging in there. Thanks for asking. And thanks again for that bowl of soup." He motioned toward a chair. "Are you ready to get to work?"

She got the message loud and clear—he appreciated the previous night, but he was all about business now. Okay, she could do business mode.

He said, "I was looking up home cooking content on YouTube and Instagram last night, and I think you're on to a winner with your Table for One idea."

"Actually, about that... I've changed my mind." She sat in the chair opposite his desk.

"Oh?" He searched her face. "Changed your mind about what?"

"About Table for One. I've decided to shelve that for the moment, and focus on content about healthy animal treats. Specifically, homemade healthy cat snacks."

"Okay," he said slowly, sitting on the edge of his desk. "That's quite a pivot."

"I know. A lot has happened since our last meeting, and this huge opportunity fell into my lap."

His eyebrows lifted. "I'd love to hear about it."

"I'm still pinching myself about how it's all coming together. I've been talking with a pet food supplement company called Nutrivite. They make vitamins for all kinds of pets. I have a few cat-related videos they liked and said they might be interested in sponsoring my YouTube channel if I made more content like that. We had a long video conference yesterday, and they offered to pay me if I mention their products in my next ten videos. They'll increase the fee if I make videos with recipes featuring their supplements. Isn't that amazing?"

He stroked his chin. "That does sound like a great opportunity."

"I know!" Johanna grinned. "And I was looking up stats on pet-related videos. They're even more promising than cooking channels. There aren't many people who are doing both. If I make videos with pet-friendly recipes, I could get a lot of revenue from advertising in addition to what Nutrivite pays. So I want to focus on this niche instead."

Gunnar walked around his desk and sat in his chair. "I'm curious. If you had a sponsor for your Table for One videos, would you still choose to focus on cat treats?"

"But I don't have a sponsor for solo meals at home. I have one who's interested in cat snacks."

"Consider this, just for the sake of argument." He propped his elbows on the polished veneer of his desk, forming a steeple with his fingers. "Imagine a sponsor came up to you and said they love the idea of a Table for One channel and want to support your content. They're willing to pay just as much as the pet supplement people. Which type of content would you rather spend your time and energy making?"

Johanna knew the answer, but didn't want to admit it. "Table for One."

"In that case, whether you have a sponsor or not, shouldn't you concentrate on the idea that has you more excited?"

"But I *am* excited about cat treats. I made a few videos about that long before I even thought about monetizing my channel." There was no need to bring up that she had fewer than ten cat recipe videos, as opposed to over two hundred that were directly related to meals for one. She hadn't thought about making more until Anton brought up Nutrivite.

"Sponsors come and go," Gunnar said. "It's not a good idea to change your entire niche because of one sponsor."

"But I've already given my word about ten videos. I can't go back on that now."

Gunnar scanned her face with his probing blue gaze. "What's really behind this change? It's not just about the sponsor, is it?"

He was way too perceptive. She forced herself to hold his gaze, heat scorching her cheeks. "A former client and his father wanted to help give my business a leg up. They put their name on the line and recommended my channel to Nutrivite. I don't want to let them down."

"Okay." He looked at his hands for a moment. Turning back to face her, he leaned forward in his chair. "When I asked what gets you fired up about sharing home-cooked food on social media, you said you wanted to spread the message that mealtimes should be special, even when you're just cook-ing for yourself."

Her jaw dropped open. How could he remember that without even looking at his notes?

His gaze never left her face. "Your Table for One idea springs from something you believe in your core. You need that kind of passion to keep you going when things get hard. And, believe me, they will get hard when your living depends on it and it's not just a hobby. Do you have that same passion for making cat treats? It might be a very good idea. But does it fit in with your vision?"

She crossed her arms. "Can't I have more than one vision?"

"Of course you can. But is this really your vision?"

She didn't answer.

Gunnar slid his glasses off and massaged the bridge of his nose. "Johanna. I have nothing against cat treats. In fact, it might be an extremely profitable niche. But you'll be making a lot of content, living and breathing this stuff for months, or even years. Burnout is a real danger for people running their own business, even when you're doing something you're fully passionate about."

He looked her full in the face again. "I've seen so many entrepreneurs come to resent their business and feel just as trapped as they did in jobs they were hoping to escape. I don't want that for you. So, if you're making this decision because you feel like you owe someone a favor and you're worried about disappointing them—"

"No, absolutely not." She couldn't meet his gaze anymore. "I love cats and I think it'll be fun to make recipe videos about cat treats. I want us to continue working on my business plan based on that."

A heavy silence fell between them until she forced herself to face him again.

He turned his gaze away and put his glasses back on. "All right. My job is to support you, but you're in the driver's seat. It sounds like your mind is made up, so let's focus on your next steps and how to build your long-term business strategy."

Johanna leaned back in her chair and watched Gunnar tap on his keyboard. He was going to help her plan her business based on content for pet treats. She had secured a deal with a corporate sponsor, and Anton and his father would be happy about how she was moving forward. So why did she feel so deflated?

Chapter 19

OHANNA CUT A GENEROUS slice of fresh cinnamon cake and slid it onto a plate. She reached for her phone to snap a picture, then remembered. Her Instagram wasn't about people food anymore.

She set the plate in front of Gunnar, who was sitting at her breakfast bar with a cup of coffee. "It's a bit too early in the year for cinnamon cake, but I made this about an hour ago. It's one of my favorites."

Gunnar sniffed appreciatively. "It smells delicious. And I agree—this is wonderful all year round." He put a bite into his mouth, closing his eyes as the fork went in.

Johanna smiled at the expression on his face. "My mother used to call cinnamon cake a hug on a plate."

Gunnar's eyes snapped open. "A hug on a plate? I can see why. This really is incredible."

What would it be like to hug Gunnar? The image popped into her head, heating her face.

She cleared her throat. "So, what are we doing in today's session? And do you normally coach your business clients in their kitchens?"

He smiled around a mouthful of cake, then took a sip of coffee. "I like to have the third session in my client's office. And I guess this counts as yours. Okay, let's begin."

He put his laptop on the counter. "You intend to build your business around creating homemade cat food. I want us to develop your elevator pitch."

"What's that?"

"It's a short summary of what your business does, who it's for, and what makes it different from the other businesses who might be doing something similar. It's supposed to be short enough so you can explain your business to a stranger while riding in an elevator."

Johanna rested her elbows on the counter. "Okay, I see."

"We won't worry about making it perfect just yet, but I like to at least give it some thought. So, your business is about sharing homemade cat food recipes online. Let's begin from there."

She held up a finger. "We'll have to refine that a bit. When I was doing my research, I found that many vets don't recommend that cats eat homemade food. There's a risk that they won't be getting all the nutrients they need. Since I don't have any formal qualifications, I think I might have to steer clear of actual meals."

"I see." He tapped on his chin. "So, what do you suggest?"

"I was thinking I'll just keep the focus on cat treats, not meals. Then all I have to do is make sure the ingredients aren't toxic and that cats love them in small amounts."

"That's a good idea. You already have a couple of videos that are doing really well."

"Yes." Her handful of videos had racked up almost three million views on YouTube the last time she checked. "And with treats, it's easier to add the Nutrivite supplements."

He glanced at her. "We'll come to Nutrivite in a couple of minutes. So, your business shares recipes for homemade cat treats. Who is it for?"

She shrugged. "Cat owners?"

"You'll have to narrow that down a bit because not every cat owner will be making treats."

"Okay, cat owners who want to learn how to make treats for their cats."

He typed on his laptop. "And what makes you different from other people who are doing something similar?"

Johanna scratched her head. That wasn't so easy to identify. "I'm not sure. When I make people food, I develop my own recipes. I taste the food myself and I can tell which recipes work. But when I make cat food, I depend on Cleo to taste what I make, and she's not the most reliable critic."

He raised an eyebrow. "Oh? What do you mean?"

"She's a bit finicky. She might turn her nose up at something that another cat absolutely loves. Or she sometimes develops a weird taste for a food that other cats hate. But she's the only way I have to gage whether the recipe tastes any good. I need to be able to film her absolutely loving the treat or else the recipe loses its credibility. You know what I mean?"

He nodded. "That is a bit of a problem."

"And then there's the Nutrivite supplements. Cleo hates them."

Gunnar stared at her. "What, all of them?"

"All the ones I've tried. I'll add just a tiny drop to her favorite food, and she refuses to eat one bite. It's the same with the treats. So, you can imagine that's a bit of a problem when I'm supposed to make these ten recipe videos. One whiff of the supplements, and she's off. I tried it with another batch of tuna treats and she fled. I haven't seen her all morning."

He smiled sheepishly. "I don't think it's only the tuna treats. She's discovered the underfloor heating in my lounge. I'm a bit spoiled and keep it on all year round. She was lying down and I couldn't budge her. Sorry I forgot to mention she was there—I hope you don't mind."

She laughed. "Underfloor heating? You'll never get her to move out now. Anyway, I didn't mean to vent. You're supposed to be helping me make a business plan and not troubleshoot my recipe issues with Nutrivite."

"No, that's fine. It actually brings me to another point. You'll have to eventually move beyond sponsorship and add other streams of income. Sponsor-based income is very unreliable."

Johanna nodded. "That's right, you talked about that before." He had mentioned her having a subscription type place where people would pay to get her recipe videos. Or writing a recipe book. "The thing is, though, I'm only just starting out making cat treats. I can't imagine anyone would want to pay me for recipes that I've only just come to grips with myself. I wouldn't feel right doing that."

He rubbed his forehead. "We'll have to give that more thought, then. I strongly advise against trying to build your livelihood on just sponsor income."

Johanna sighed.

"Could you make the treats to sell at craft fairs?" he asked.

"I guess I could. But that's a whole other dimension. I've never thought remotely about that. To be honest, I'm not even sure I want to."

"Fair enough." He looked at her. "All we have down here, then, is sponsorship. Either from YouTube ad revenue or another business like Nutrivite."

Johanna bit her lip. "And you said sponsorship isn't sustainable in the long term."

"I said it wasn't stable. You could sustain it if you keep making content and bringing in viewers and subscribers. But your income would fluctuate. You would also be dependent on YouTube. What happens if YouTube goes away like MySpace?"

"That's a scary thought."

"We don't need to figure it out right this minute. There are other options out there."

She had felt so much more excitement with her Table for One idea. The ideas had flowed, and the potential seemed limitless. With cat treats, though, everything seemed much harder, down to the most basic building block of coming up with the recipes themselves.

Her viewing numbers were great—people were clearly loving her cat treats content. But she didn't feel the same buzz as when she'd been working on her Table for One idea. Was this what Gunnar had been talking about when he mentioned being fired up about her work?

Maybe it was something she'd grow into as she became more familiar with the new niche. But what if she didn't?

She had to make it work, though. Nutrivite was delighted with her numbers, and so were Anton and Mr. Erlandson.

Her face must have reflected something, because Gunnar said, "I know it feels overwhelming, but you've got this. Just take it step by step."

She stretched her lips into a smile. Although he'd questioned her hard about this pivot, he was doing his best to help her.

But what if he'd been right about this being the wrong niche for her?

Chapter 20

JOHANNA ADDED AN EXTRA squeeze of lime juice to her char-grilled zucchini and ricotta salad. The dish was already perfect and more lime would just upset the balance, but her hands needed something to do.

Reidun sidled up, a glass of lemonade in her hand. "So, are we still waiting for your mystery guest? I think everyone's hungry, but they're too polite to say so."

Trust Reidun to bring up the uncomfortable truth. It was well after three on Saturday afternoon, and Johanna had prepared to serve lunch by half-past one. All the food was ready, but Anton wasn't here yet.

She glanced through the French doors at her friends, who sat in loose groups around her patio.

Lukas and Bethany were here, along with Lukas's brother Kai and his wife, Lisa. She'd given Gunnar an invite via a note slipped into his mailbox a couple of days ago. These were all his friends, too, and since he lived next door, it might look strange if she didn't at least ask him. He sat chatting with Kai, Cleo sprawled on his lap.

Johanna tossed the squeezed out lime into the bin. "Okay, I'll serve lunch." She couldn't wait for Anton any longer.

"Finally." Reidun threw her hands in the air. "Do you need any help?"

"Yes, please. I've got some chicken skewers keeping warm in the oven along with the spareribs. Would you mind putting them on these platters?"

As Reidun got to work, Johanna grabbed a package of burger buns. The patties had been cooked ages ago and were warm in a chafing dish.

Where was Anton? She'd made it clear that they were starting at one o'clock. At least no one other than Reidun knew she was waiting for one more guest. They'd just think she was running late with the meal.

When she brought the food out, it was clear Reidun was right about the guests being hungry. Everyone took generous helpings.

Lukas dived into his plate, moaning as he chewed a piece of chicken. "This is incredible, Johanna. How do you do it?"

"I know, right?" Reidun said. "Even when I follow your instructions step by step, my food turns out nothing like yours. You need to make a cooking for dummies livestream where you can show us how to turn the kettle on."

Bethany swiped a napkin across her mouth. "I tried the chocolate soufflé recipe you uploaded a couple of days ago. I'd never made one before, but it turned out perfect. Did you say you were going to make one about raspberry soufflé this week? I can't wait to try that, too."

Oh, right, the raspberry soufflé. Johanna winced. That got lost in the shuffle after her meeting with Anton and his father. "It's been a busy week. But, you're right, I did promise that."

She glanced at Gunnar, but he was focused on the mechanics of eating a burger with Cleo stretched out on his lap. She was going to have to tell her friends and her viewing audience that her focus going forward would be on making treats for cats. Her thoughts had so far been about all the new viewers she'd be getting. She hadn't considered her existing followers—people who wanted her regular recipes and weren't interested in cooking for their pets.

Johanna got a plate and served herself some salad and a couple of chicken skewers. As she headed to her seat, a black Jaguar glided down the road. Anton had finally arrived.

Johanna put her plate on the table. "Excuse me."

It would be quicker to cross the yard than to go through the house to the front door. Cleo hopped down and followed Johanna as she crossed the grass and met Anton on the front porch.

Cleo went rigid, her ears flattening against her head. Staring at Anton, she hissed with her sharp teeth exposed, then darted off toward Gunnar's house.

Anton watched her bolt away. "What's wrong with that cat? I can't believe it's the same one in your videos. In real life, it's more like the Tasmanian Devil."

"I don't know. She was fine a second ago." Johanna could just make out the cat's shape under a chair on Gunnar's porch. She faced Anton. "I'm glad you made it."

She paused, waiting for an apology for his lateness, but it didn't come. Finally she said, "Shall we go and join everyone else? We're sitting in the backyard, and we've just started eating."

Several gazes turned to Anton as he and Johanna stepped onto the patio.

"Everyone, this is Anton Einarson. He lives over in Havdal."

Johanna caught the lift in Gunnar's eyebrows when she mentioned Anton's name. He was probably putting two and two together with the conversation they'd had earlier that week.

Anton raised a hand in greeting. "Hi, everyone."

Reidun gestured at the table. "We're all going to be rather antisocial while we eat this amazing food. You'd better grab a plate while there's still any left."

Anton patted his stomach. "I'm good, thanks. I just ate." He chose a seat near Gunnar.

Johanna stared at him. He just ate? When she'd invited him over for lunch? That was probably why he was so late. But why hadn't he let her know he'd be delayed? She'd held up the meal and let her friends sit here hungry while he was eating somewhere else.

She squashed down her annoyance. There must have been a good reason. "Maybe you can have some dessert later. Do you want a drink? We have fruit juices, sodas, or iced tea."

He made a face. "I'd rather have a cup of coffee, please. A cappuccino, if you don't mind."

"Okay. I'll be right back." Her gaze drifted over her still full plate that sat on the table, and her empty stomach complained.

In the kitchen, she set about making Anton's cappuccino.

Reidun came in with an empty plate as Johanna was frothing the milk with the steaming wand from her espresso machine.

Reidun put the plate next to the sink. "So, this Anton guy strolls in over an hour late. He's already eaten, but he asks you to make him a cappuccino so you have to delay your own meal even longer."

Johanna shrugged. "I'll be done in a couple of minutes."

"How did he even know you could make him a cappuccino at home? An espresso machine isn't exactly a common household item." Reidun hooked her thumbs into the waistband of her jeans. "He must have been here before. Are you guys together?"

Heat crept up Johanna's neck. "I wouldn't quite say that. But we're exploring the possibility."

"Where does he go to church?"

"He attends the Free Church in Havdal." She shot Reidun a look. "I learned my lesson after Hans, okay? I wouldn't even be considering dating a man who didn't have a profession of faith."

Johanna poured the foamed milk into the cup of espresso, swirling it around until it formed a perfect cap of milky froth. "There. Making the cappuccino didn't take that long."

Reidun didn't reply, but followed Johanna as she took the cup out to Anton. He had turned his back on Gunnar and was now chatting with Lukas and Bethany.

He took the drink from her. "Thank you. I love how you make these."

Her face heated up again at Bethany's questioning glance. She retrieved her plate of now cold chicken skewers and went back to where Anton sat.

Lukas looked at her. "I can't get over your zucchini and ricotta salad. Do you have the recipe on your YouTube channel?"

"I'm not sure, but I don't think I have this particular recipe."

"Could you pretty please consider uploading it?"

Bethany held up her fork. "Hey, she needs to do the raspberry soufflé first."

"Actually, I think she's going to be pretty busy making snacks for her cat." Anton sipped his cappuccino as several gazes whipped toward him.

He smirked and winked at Johanna.

"Snacks for your cat?" Bethany repeated.

"Oh, it's just a business thing." Johanna waved her hand. "I'm partnering with one of Anton's associates to make recipes for cat-friendly snacks. I'll be hitting that pretty hard going forward, so there won't be as many people food videos."

"Oh, wow. That sounds very exciting," Bethany said. "Congratulations."

Lukas echoed his wife. "Yeah, congratulations."

A lull in the conversation followed, mercifully broken by a ring tone.

Anton pulled out his phone. "Excuse me. Hello?" He stood and walked a few feet away, phone pressed to his ear.

Reidun jumped to her feet. "I'll help you with dessert now, Johanna."

Johanna stared at her. She was still eating her cold chicken and wasn't quite ready to serve dessert, but Reidun was striding into the house.

Johanna put her plate down and followed her friend.

In the kitchen, Reidun spun around to face her. "Let's go look in your closet."

"Have you lost your mind? I thought you wanted dessert, but now you want to check out my closet?"

"Humor me." Reidun turned around. "Come on. Let's go."

Johanna shook her head. This was strange, even for Reidun.

They went into the hallway and Reidun pulled open the closet door. "Let's see. Ah, there they are. Your fishing tackle and life jacket. You got that when you were dating Ivan and he was into salmon fishing."

Johanna folded her arms. "You are making zero sense, and I don't have time for this. I've got guests waiting for dessert."

"No, no, hang on a minute." Reidun pushed her head deeper into the closet and rummaged around. "Where are your oil painting supplies? Never mind. This will prove my point, too."

She pulled out an acoustic guitar in its black case. "This dates back to the Jonas era. You took up guitar lessons because he was your boyfriend and that's what he was doing at the time. That was just before you dated Karl and got into painting."

"Why are you bringing all this up? Because I've dated a few guys?"

Reidun put her hands on her hips. "No, it's not because you've dated guys. Who hasn't? You're forty-seven—of course you've had a few relationships. It's not that. But each time you're interested in a guy, you've morphed your life like a chameleon in order to fit in with his interests. I really began to see it after you sold your perfectly good Toyota and bought that 1960s MGB Roadster."

Johanna clenched her fists. A former boyfriend, Petter, was heavily into classic cars. She'd thought getting the Roadster would help them bond while spending time together at car shows and going on long drives in the summer.

Reidun leaned on the closet door. "The only hobby you've stuck to was cooking, and then your blog and YouTube channel. It's your happy place, and it made so much sense that you were making a career out of it. And now Anton comes along and you're suddenly shunting that aside to focus on cat treats. Why do you let these guys have so much power over you?"

Heat swept through Johanna's body. "You have no idea what you're talking about." She spun on her heel and stalked to the kitchen.

She yanked open the fridge door and dragged a cheesecake out. Her decision to focus on pet-related content was based on business principles. But her friend's words rankled.

Johanna ran through a mental list of the men she'd dated over the years. There was Timothy, who'd had his heart set on becoming a missionary in

East Africa. She'd started learning Swahili even though they were only dating casually.

She'd briefly dabbled in veganism when she'd dated a guy for nine months. What was his name again? While they were together, she'd thrown out all her leather bags and shoes and gotten rid of all her woolen garments and accessories. That had been a miserable winter. And all for a guy whose name she couldn't even remember. Reidun had forgotten that one, thank goodness.

Johanna put a tray of brownies onto the worktop. It landed with a clatter. Gripping the edge of the counter, she squeezed her eyes shut.

A hand touched her arm.

"I didn't mean to make you mad," Reidun said. "Years ago, Bethany made a comment about how you'd given up your lovely new car and bought a heap of junk just because you were dating a guy who loved to restore classic cars."

"What, you mean you've been talking about me?"

"It was just one comment. But it made me realize you've done the same thing ever since I've known you. When you like a guy, Johanna, you tend to let his every whim guide your decisions. Your boyfriend says jump and you go out and buy a trampoline. And now you're changing your entire business focus because of a collaboration with Anton's friend."

Bethany walked in from the patio, carrying a load of dirty dishes. "What's going on here?"

Reidun slanted a glance at Johanna. "I'm doing an intervention."

"And I'm going to serve dessert," Johanna said.

Bethany put the dishes on the counter. "What's the intervention about?"

"Anton. It's the classic cars all over again."

"Ah," Bethany said.

"I need both of you to drop it." Johanna put the desserts onto a large tray. She opened a cupboard and grabbed a stack of side plates. "If you want to help me, please take these plates out."

Her friends exchanged a look and held their silence.

Johanna went out with the desserts.

Anton walked toward her, his phone still in his hand. "Hey, I'm really sorry about this, but my father just called. He needs me to step in and take some out-of-town business associates to dinner. I need to leave now."

"Oh. Okay. That's too bad." She put the tray onto the table.

Anton swept his gaze around the patio and stepped forward. He leaned toward her and pitched his voice to a low murmur. "It'd be great if you could come, too. Would you be able to wrap things up here in the next half hour or so?"

Was he seriously suggesting that she stop lunch now? "I have guests. I can't just ask my friends to leave."

He shrugged. "I thought it might be a good chance for you to meet my friends. Anyway, I'd better go now. I'll call you."

Raising his voice, he waved a hand. "It was nice meeting you all. Bye." He started off across the yard.

Johanna hadn't quite set up the dessert things for her friends. She glanced at Anton's retreating form and then back down at the tray of brownies.

Reidun stepped up beside her. "I'll sort this dessert out. See your friend off."

Johanna glanced at Reidun. "Thanks." She followed Anton across the yard.

Chapter 21

WHY HAD HE EVEN come here today? Gunnar's gaze strayed after Johanna as she followed Anton across the yard. It shouldn't surprise him that she was involved with someone. But why did it have to be someone so smug and self-satisfied?

Johanna was warm-hearted and empathetic—the sort of woman for whom kindness was an instinct. He'd seen that on the night he'd told her about his mother. Anton would soak all that up like it was his due. The guy had been here fifteen minutes and done nothing but talk about himself to people he was meeting for the first time.

It also rankled that this Anton was behind Johanna's sudden pivot in her business focus. This was the fellow she didn't want to disappoint, for whom she was putting aside the content he knew she really wanted to do?

Gunnar caught the train of his thoughts and wrestled them back under control. Who Johanna Strand dated was none of his business. She was his client and his neighbor, and they had some friends in common. That was all.

The sleek black Jaguar started with a growl, mounting to a roar as it peeled out of the driveway.

He watched Johanna as Anton drove off, tearing his gaze away when Reidun offered him a brownie. "Or would you rather have some cheesecake? Both made by Johanna's own fair hands."

Gunnar looked up at her. "Cheesecake, please. Or, you know what? I'm actually pretty full, so I'll skip dessert and head back home. I need to catch up on some work." Like fast-tracking his writeup of Johanna's business plan so he could be done with their contract. He did not want a ringside seat to her business or her personal life any more than he had to, especially when both involved Anton.

"Aw, too bad," Reidun said. "I was hoping to pick your brain about this Anton fellow."

Gunnar stood. "I know nothing about him." Apart from the fact that, thanks to his influence, Johanna was going to drop a perfectly viable business she loved and rebuild an untested one from scratch.

Reidun opened her mouth as though to say something else, but Johanna came back.

"Thanks for lunch," Gunnar said.

Johanna's eyes widened. "Oh, you're leaving?"

"Yeah. There are things I need to get done. Bye."

He said a quick goodbye to his friends and went back home.

He would put in a solid couple of hours' work and then go for a run. By the time he was done, his mind would be settled. Work and heavy exercise had done wonders in the past.

He went straight to his computer and booted it up, freezing as a message notification popped up on his screen. Stefan had replied to his email.

Chapter 22

HIS FINGERS STIFF, GUNNAR opened the email from his brother, devouring the lines.

Hi, Gunnar.

I was expecting to hear from you, although it was still something of a shock when your message came.

I agree it's important that Mamma and Pappa have a special celebration. That's why I offered to host it. If it means you being there, I won't stand in the way of that happening.

Don't stay away on my account.

Stefan

Gunnar read the note several times over, weighing its words, trying to distill the tone. His brother was still angry. The terseness of the last few sentences showed that. The only reason Stefan would tolerate his presence was because their parents wanted it.

Reconciliation with Stefan might be too much to ask for, but at least Mamma would have all her children at the anniversary party.

Breathing a prayer of thanks, he dialed Maria's number.

"Stefan just sent me an email," he said as soon as she picked up.

"What did he say?"

"He says it's okay for me to come to the party."

Maria squealed. "That's fantastic news. Mamma will be so happy. When will you come down?"

Gunnar pulled up the calendar on his computer. "Let's see, the party is a week from today. I would have liked to come a couple of days early, but I need to wind up a project with a client. I'll book a flight and get there on Saturday morning."

Since Stefan was playing host, it probably wouldn't be a good idea for Gunnar to outstretch his welcome by arriving too early. He'd make an appearance for the party and find a different time to visit with Mamma and Pappa.

"It'll be so good to see you."

"Same," Gunnar said. "Sorry I won't be able to help much setting anything up."

"That's fine. The caterers are all arranged. What you could do is play chauffeur for Mamma and Pappa. Drive them to the party and back home when it's over."

"Sure. I'm happy to do that."

"I'm so glad this is going to work out," Maria said. "See you in a week."

Gunnar ended the call.

Before he left for Trondheim, he needed to deliver that business plan to Johanna. Even though his gut told him she was making a mistake with her change of focus, he'd hold his nose and write the best plan he could. And then he'd draw a line under his work with her. He often offered follow-up consultations with his clients, but he would not do that for Johanna.

He needed to keep his distance from her. His reaction to Anton told him that. He was not going to let himself fall for a woman who was involved with someone else. Never again.

Chapter 23

ANTON WASN'T EVEN HERE yet, but Johanna wanted the evening to be over.

It was the first time they would spend time alone since he'd first suggested they begin seeing each other. But ever since the barbecue, she'd known something was off, like a false note intruding on an otherwise harmonious chord.

Still, she went through the motions, decorating the table, dressing, and choosing the menu with care. Perhaps things would be clearer after tonight.

She'd decided to serve Steak Diane along with a radish and watercress salad. Their dessert, sticky toffee pudding, was in the oven and should be ready to come out in about five minutes. The salad was already done, but she wouldn't start on the steak until Anton was here. The seasoned beef tenderloin sat on the kitchen counter, and she'd already mixed up the ingredients for the sauce.

Hopefully, Cleo wouldn't act like a hellcat tonight. Where was she, anyway? Johanna glanced around the room. She was probably hanging out at Gunnar's place, enjoying his heated floors. Johanna was a lot more relaxed now about Cleo spending time next door. Come to think of it, Gunnar was another person she hadn't seen in a while.

A movement flashed in the corner of her eye and, looking out of her front window, she saw Anton's Jaguar sliding into her driveway.

He met her at the door with a bouquet of roses and peonies. He leaned forward and kissed her cheek. "Hello, gorgeous. These are for you."

"Thanks. Please come in."

He walked after her into the hallway. "Mm, something smells delicious. What are we having?"

She smiled at him over her shoulder. "Steak Diane with watercress salad and sticky toffee pudding. I hope you brought your appetite."

"Always."

"Something to drink?"

"I'll have a club soda."

Johanna poured him the drink, then joined him in the living room.

He sat sprawled with his arm draped on the back of the sofa. "Why don't you join me over here?"

She put the drink on the coffee table in front of him. "I need to put the flowers in water." The thought of cozying up next to him did not appeal to her as much as it would have a few days ago.

He took a deep sip of his drink. "I needed that. It's been a long day. How are things going for you? Post any more viral content?"

"I've been doing some market research and trying to come up with ideas for new cat treat recipes. To be honest, I'm a bit worried." She took her time unwrapping the bouquet.

"Worried? What do you have to be worried about?"

"The videos are supposed to show me making treats for my cat. But Cleo hates the Nutrivite supplements. I've tried with every item in their cat catalog, but she won't touch any food it's in. I don't know whether it's just her or if it's a problem with the product itself."

Anton rolled his eyes. "That cat of yours is certifiably insane."

Johanna's hackles rose. "There's nothing wrong with Cleo. I think I might have been too quick to agree to the sponsorship with Nutrivite."

"What are you talking about? It's a wonderful partnership. They've offered you such great terms. Why don't you try another cat?"

"Try another cat? Excuse me?"

"Why not?"

He could not be serious. "I'm not getting an entire new cat just for the sake of a vitamin supplement."

Anton rolled his eyes. "Fine. Keep your cat. Who said you actually have to put the supplements in your recipe?"

"What?"

"You just said your cat was finicky. Chances are, a normal cat would have no problem with Nutrivite's stuff. The company would have run out of business if their supplements taste that bad. So, we can conclude that your cat is the exception and other normal cats don't mind it. And if that's the case, just make a regular treat and feed that to your cat. Film that, and boom. Video done."

Johanna stared at him. "But that would be deceptive. I couldn't do that."

"I don't see anything wrong with it. It's no more deceptive than ads that use special visual effects. There's no need to be precious about it."

She shook her head. "That's not how I want to operate my business."

"Are you always this pedantic or is this the kind of thing that two-bit business consultant of yours has been teaching you?" he sneered.

Anger flared within her. "Gunnar is a well-respected consultant, and he's encouraged me to follow my instincts.

He's done nothing but support my decisions."

"It's just because he knows which side his bread is buttered. You're paying him, so of course he's going to say what he thinks you want to hear."

Johanna saw red. At least Gunnar was building a career off his own back rather than riding on his father's coattails like Anton was. She clenched her fists in her effort to keep her thoughts from spilling out of her mouth.

When she could trust her voice, she said, "I'm going to pull out of the collaboration with Nutrivite. I have two more videos to upload, but those will be the last."

Anton sat up, throwing up his hands. "I thought you were smarter than this. You're making the amateur mistake of believing that chances like this come along every day just because you got this offer very early on."

"I know it's a very good opportunity and I'm grateful to you for making it happen, but it's just not what I want to do."

He looked her up and down. "My father will be very disappointed. He put his name on the line to back you for this. We really misjudged you."

Her face burned. "Once again, thanks for the opportunity. But it's not right for me."

"I don't have time for this." He stood. "I'll see myself out. And Johanna..." he gave her a long stare. "Don't bother to call me."

He strode down the hallway. The door swished and a loud bang sounded.

Johanna snatched his wretched bouquet and threw the flowers into the trash can. He wasn't the only one guilty of misjudging. So, that was that. She'd better email Nutrivite before word got to them through Anton. It was only right that the news come from her.

She pulled out her laptop and sent an email to her contact in Nutrivite, her heart immediately lifting as she hit the send button. There. She felt free again, and in charge of her own destiny.

Her glance fell on the raw steaks on the kitchen counter, seasoned and ready to cook. She'd better put them back in the fridge.

A whiff of something scorched hit her nose. The sticky toffee pudding! She dashed to the oven and pulled out the singed mess. There was no way to salvage it. She'd better take it outside before it set off a smoke alarm.

She took the smoking tin outside the back door and onto her patio. Her gaze collided with Gunnar's.

He was sitting on his deck with his laptop. He waved in greeting. "What's up?"

"Baking disaster." She raised the cake tin. "I had to bring it outside before all the smoke alarms start ringing."

She put the tin down and looked around. "Cleo must really love your new deck. Or is it the underfloor heating in your lounge? I haven't seen her in ages."

Gunnar frowned. "Cleo? I haven't seen her in days. Not since your barbecue."

"What?" Johanna's heart lurched. "She's not turned up at your place? The last time I saw her was..." she did a mental calculation. "More than five days ago."

Her body went cold. Cleo was missing.

Chapter 24

ARK THOUGHTS SWIRLED THROUGH Johanna's mind. Cleo run over by a car, or perhaps attacked again, this time with no Good Samaritan to take her to the vet in time. "Do you think she's—" her mouth refused to give voice to her fears.

Gunnar got to his feet. He was on her patio in a few quick strides. "There's no need to imagine the worst. Cleo's probably found another nice home to hang out in. We could ask around and check whether anybody's seen her. If you make 'missing' posters, I'll help you put them around the neighborhood."

"Okay." She made herself take several slow breaths. Gunnar was right. "I'll put a post on Facebook as well."

He followed her inside her house, glancing at the table set for two, but making no comment.

She fired up her laptop and in a few minutes, she slapped together a poster with Cleo's picture, the words "missing," and her phone number at the bottom.

Gunnar stood next to the printer as it ran several dozen copies of the poster. Grabbing them, he looked across at Johanna. "I'll put these up on Elvegata, Esbensensgata, and the corner shop. You can put some here on Nyborgveien."

Johanna nodded. It made sense to put the posters on the two roads that ran parallel to theirs. "Maybe I should take a poster to the noticeboard over at the supermarket."

"Good thinking."

Johanna took a handful of posters from him.

He rubbed his chin. "On second thought, maybe it would be better if I put up all the posters and you could go door to door and ask people whether they've seen Cleo. Wait. If you make the posters a bit smaller, like flyers, we could put them in people's mailboxes."

Johanna liked the idea of going door to door. It was more immediate than

waiting on the off chance that someone might read a poster on a lamp-
post. "I'll make some flyers now."

When that was done, Gunnar headed westward along the street with a stapler and his pile of posters and flyers while she started with the neighbor to the right of her house.

She was on smiling and waving terms with the family of two tweens and their mother, but they didn't talk much. One of the children—a boy of around eleven—answered the door and said he hadn't seen Cleo. He took a flyer, saying he'd ask his sister when she came home from soccer practice.

The people in the next two homes were away, but Johanna left flyers in their mailboxes.

She started on the other side of the street, glimpsing Gunnar putting up a poster on the bulletin board at the small playground between house numbers seven and five. He'd dropped everything to help her. She'd have to do something to thank him. Maybe a basket of muffins.

None of the neighbors she spoke to on her street had seen Cleo recently, so Johanna went to Elvegata, the next road over. Cleo sometimes wandered around here.

The first two houses were of no help, and anxiety churned Johanna's gut. It wasn't a good sign that no one had seen Cleo in so long.

She knocked on the third door in the street.

The dark red door swung open and a woman in her mid-thirties peered out. Her face was unfamiliar. They must have moved in recently. Johanna remembered the "for sale" sign that had stood outside this property for a couple of months.

She mustered a smile. "Hello. I'm sorry to bother you. I'm Johanna and I live just over there on Nyborgveien. My cat has gone missing, and I wonder whether you might have seen her."

Johanna held out a flyer.

The woman barely glanced at it. "I'm not entirely sure."

Johanna caught a flicker in the woman's blue eyes. "But you might have? Please, have another look. I haven't seen her in a few days and I'm worried sick." She held out the flyer again.

The woman folded her toned arms across her chest. "I don't know how worried you could really be. Fine, I have seen that cat. She's been here for the past five days. We couldn't understand why no one had come looking for her in all that time, and she didn't seem inclined to go anywhere else, either."

Johanna's heart leaped. "You've seen her? Where is she? Is she okay?"

"She's here, like I said. She walked in here during a rainstorm, poor thing, cold and shivering. She was really hungry, too. We gave her a meal and thought she might want to go back home, but she just seemed to want to stay. We were wondering what kind of owners would be content to let their cat stay out for so many days without looking for her. Where we come from, people start putting up posters within a couple of days if their cat doesn't come home."

Johanna's ears burned. "I didn't know she was missing."

"You didn't know she was missing," the woman repeated, lifting her chin. "How can you not know that your own cat was missing for almost a week?"

Who was this woman to judge her pet parenting skills? All the same, Johanna felt a need to justify herself. "Cleo often spends time with my neighbor, so I thought that's where she was, okay? That's why it took me a while to realize that neither of us has seen her."

"Your neighbor? If she's your cat, why does she need to take refuge in someone else's place?"

Johanna had had enough of this woman's insinuations. "Listen, I'm not here to debate how I treat my pet. Cleo is perfectly healthy and happy. Could you please hand her over now?"

"How do I even know she's your cat?"

"Excuse me?" Johanna stared at the woman. Had she walked into some parallel dimension?

The woman propped her hands on her hips. "For all I know, you might be trying to kidnap her. Can you show me proof that she's your cat?"

Johanna took in a deep, deliberate breath, praying for the willpower not to throttle this woman. She blew the air out slowly. "Cleo is my cat. I have photographic evidence, receipts, and she's micro-chipped. If you don't hand her over right now, I'm going to contact the police and accuse you of theft."

A vast man loomed behind the cat woman. He glowered at Johanna. "Watch your tone with my wife. What is this about?"

The woman turned to face her husband. "She claims that Mittens is hers."

Mittens? They'd had the audacity to rename her cat?

"Ah." The man and his wife stared at Johanna with matching his and hers judgy faces. He jabbed a beefy finger in her face. "You let your cat wander around for a week before you come looking for her, and then you have the nerve to harass the woman who's fed and housed her and kept her safe all this time?"

"Listen here—"

"Hey Johanna, I've finished putting flyers around this road. What's up here?" Gunnar jogged up to her.

"They have Cleo," Johanna said. She stopped short. If she said another word, she might burst into angry tears and embarrass herself.

"Is that right?" Gunnar's tone was over the top enthusiastic. "Cleo is safe? Thanks so much for taking care of that little rascal. She comes and goes at will between a few of the neighborhood homes, so it took us a while to realize none of us had seen her. We'll take her off your hands now, unless there's anything else."

Whether it was because he was a man or because they just liked Gunnar's vibe better than hers, the couple visibly relaxed, and the woman even batted her eyelashes.

"Oh, since you're vouching for her, we're happy to release Mittens. I just wanted to be sure she had a good home. She's such a lovely cat, and the children have become so attached to her. I'll go find her."

Johanna bit her tongue to keep from replying.

Gunnar made small talk with the man, something about the Norwegian soccer league and what Rosenborg's chances were this year.

The woman came back, Cleo in her arms. "Here you go." She glared at Johanna, then made a big production of handing the cat to Gunnar. "She's welcome to visit anytime. And you can stop by for coffee, too."

Johanna gritted her teeth. Cleo would never come back here again if she could help it. She gave a curt nod to the couple and turned to walk down the road.

Gunnar said his goodbyes, then trotted up to Johanna, falling into step beside her. "Here you go, Cleo. Go back to your mom."

He smiled as Johanna took Cleo into her arms. "Thank God she's okay. I can't believe I didn't notice she was gone for all that time."

"She has been spending a lot more time at my place, so it's not strange that you didn't notice. Don't be so down on yourself."

"Thanks." It was sweet of him to try to make her feel better.

"I need to take down the posters I just put up," he said. "And I'm afraid we'll have to make 'found' flyers and leave them in all the mailboxes."

Johanna buried her face in Cleo's fur. She didn't care about the extra work. "Thanks for diffusing that situation with the cat lady and her husband. It was escalating fast. I don't know what would have happened if you hadn't shown up when you did."

"There was definitely a weird vibe. I was up the street with my flyers, and the woman's body language looked pretty confrontational, so I came closer. Then her husband showed up and I thought I'd better try to see if I could calm everyone down by being all innocent."

"It worked, thank God," Johanna said. "And thanks so much."

"No problem."

They walked for a while, cutting across the playground.

Gunnar threw her a sidelong glance. "So, did you think I was like those two? Trying to keep your cat for myself?"

She cringed. How could she have ever thought that about him? "Maybe.

A little. I feel very silly about that now."

"Having seen those two, I understand why you were a bit suspicious of me. Cat nappers are a thing, and I don't blame you for being worried. I would never have believed people like that exist."

It was a gracious thing to say, and her heart warmed.

Cleo started squirming when they reached home, so Johanna put her down.

Gunnar held out the leftover posters and flyers. "I'd better take down the others I posted."

"Thanks. I'll run up some flyers to say Cleo was found and leave them in everyone's mailboxes." She hesitated for a moment. "I've got the makings of a really good steak dinner. If you haven't eaten yet, you're welcome to join me."

"I... thanks. That sounds lovely." A light flush crept up his face.

Her pulse quickened. "Okay. Come in."

Chapter 25

GUNNAR FOLLOWED JOHANNA INSIDE. This wasn't a good idea. He enjoyed being with her too much. When he'd seen her so afraid for Cleo's safety, nothing could have stopped him from stepping in to help. Work, deadlines, schedule. Every hesitation had vanished in his impulse to take her fear away. Watching her relief at getting her cat back, his own heart had soared to giddy heights.

If he was smart, he would turn around, go home, and walk straight into a cold shower.

Johanna was with Anton. Given Gunnar's track record, the last thing he should be doing was spending time with an attractive woman who was dating someone else. He'd played with that kind of fire before, and it had exploded into a blaze that burned out of control and incinerated his life. It was why he no longer had a brother.

And yet here he was, in her house, about to eat dinner with her.

"You can sit at the dining table or the breakfast bar if you like," Johanna said. "The steaks won't take long."

It was too late to back out. He walked toward the kitchen counter, gesturing at the elegantly decorated table. "I seem to have gained from someone else's loss."

"Oh." She glanced at the table, then turned toward the sink, speaking with her back to Gunnar. "Anton was here, but he left without eating."

Her words hit him like a bucket of icy water. So, all this was for Anton—the candles, the linen napkins, porcelain and crystal tableware. But the reality check was good for him. He would not forget himself and start imagining this meal was something other than it was. "Have you been dating Anton long?"

She whirled around to look at him, color staining her tawny cheeks. "Dating? Anton and I aren't dating."

Heat washed over him. "You're not? I thought you—"

"We kind of considered it, but..." she threw her hands up. "It was one of those complicated, undefined things. But there's no question mark now. We're definitely not together after today." She turned back to the sink and soaped up her hands.

He stared at her back, conflicting emotions wrestling for place within him. If she and Anton weren't dating, was it so wrong for him to want to get closer to Johanna? But would she even want to know him if she knew what he was capable of? Images of Annette flashed through his mind.

"Actually, speaking of Anton, that reminds me." She faced him again, wiping her hands dry with a towel. "I told him today that I'm ending my collaboration with Nutrivite."

This was big news. "So, are you back to your Table for One idea?"

"Yes. The whole pet treats thing just wasn't working out." She opened the fridge and pulled out a stick of butter. "Sorry to be so flaky about all of this, but we'll have to go back to square one for the third time with my business plan. I should have just listened to you when you had your doubts."

He was dangerously pleased that she valued his opinion. It was none of his business, but he couldn't keep from asking. "Was Anton pushing you to collaborate with Nutrivite?"

She froze, a knife poised over the opened package of butter. "His father personally vouched for me and I guess they were both invested in it working out. He couldn't see why I might want to pull out."

So, reading between the lines, Anton had flounced off when Johanna decided not to work with Nutrivite. It sounded like a messy tangle of business decisions and personal feelings, and if he didn't watch himself, he'd get all snarled up into it. Especially if Johanna still had unresolved feelings for Anton.

Time to change the subject. "What are you cooking?"

"Steak Diane." She turned the heat up under a large pan and threw in a generous dollop of butter.

He could watch her cook all day. Her movements were fluid and assured, like a dancer at one with her craft.

And there went his wayward thoughts again, pushing his mind into perilous waters. He shouldn't be staring at her like this. He stood and walked over to some framed portraits on her bookshelf, stopping in front of one that showed a very young Johanna—about twelve or thirteen, if he had to guess—wearing a sports uniform and standing next to a man who had to be her father. They had the same dark eyes and open smile.

Another picture, this time an action shot, captured an older Johanna leaping in midair, arm reared back and poised to launch a handball while girls from the opposing team surrounded her, forming a barricade with their uplifted hands. In the background, Johanna's father stood at the sidelines, fists raised above his head, his yell frozen in time.

"I didn't know you were into handball," Gunnar said.

A steak sizzled as she put it onto the hot pan and then added a second piece of meat. "I was very much into it. I played in the junior league for several years and was in the national under seventeen team once. That picture over there was at the junior European women's championships the year Norway won gold, although I was on the bench most of the time. My dad had high hopes I might make the Olympic team."

"Wow, really?" There were so many sides to her he didn't know. "Why did you quit?"

"Injury. I tore a ligament in my knee. I had surgery, but it was never the same. The doctor said I couldn't play competitively again."

"I'm sorry. That must have been hard."

"You know, strange to say, it actually wasn't." She moved the steak around the pan with a pair of tongs. "I hadn't really enjoyed it in a while. My injury gave me a way out without disappointing people."

Did she mean her father? He turned back to the pictures. "Where's your dad now?"

"He passed away about five years ago."

"I'm sorry to hear that."

"Thanks."

He went back to his seat at the breakfast bar. "Do you have any siblings?"

"I have two stepsisters." She turned the steaks over. "My dad and mom got divorced when I was around eight, and he remarried a woman whose children went to my school. They were all really into handball, training three days a week, and playing matches most weekends. My dad was super keen on it, too, and he became their coach. I tried out for the team because in my ten-year-old brain I thought that'd get me more time with him."

"Did it?"

"Yup. I used to play the violin back then. Dad never had time to attend my music recitals, but he'd never miss any of my games. So, I dropped the music and concentrated on the sports."

Her sad smile tugged at his heart. That was a lot of time spent on a sport she didn't particularly enjoy. And she'd kept up with it because it was her father's thing. "Do you see much of your family?"

"My stepsisters both live in Oslo now, and their mom splits her time between there and Spain. We're friendly, but I guess it was mostly Dad and handball that we had in common." She looked up at him. "I forgot to ask how you like your steak."

"However you're having yours is fine."

"In that case, I'll take them off now. They should be medium rare." She put the steaks aside, covering them with foil.

He rested his elbows on the counter, watching her hands as she diced half a cup of shallots and tipped them into the pan.

Annette was the last woman who'd made a meal just for him. It had been delicious. He'd since learned that even deadly poison could taste exquisite.

His hands clenched into fists. Why did thoughts of Annette have to intrude, polluting every moment? Maybe that was the penance he had to pay.

It didn't matter how interested he was in Johanna. Once she knew what he was capable of, would she even want to be friends with him? There was only one way to find out. He needed to let her know what he'd done and kill any false hope before it had a chance to take root in his heart.

With the steak resting, it was time to make the sauce. Johanna whisked together beef broth, Dijon mustard, tomato paste, and Worcestershire sauce.

She glanced at Gunnar. He'd gone quiet, his gaze on the kitchen counter.

"We've done a lot of talking about me. I'd love to know more about you, too."

His head snapped up, blue eyes widening as though he'd forgotten she was there. "Sorry, what did you say?"

"I said I'd like to know more about you. Was it hard being a preacher's kid? All eyes on you, pressure to be an example, and all that."

"Not for me. I loved being involved in church stuff. I was there whenever the doors opened. My brother did struggle, though. My sister and I became Christians at quite a young age, but Stefan went through a questioning phase when he was around thirteen." His lips twisted. "He's never really come out of that phase yet."

"All we can do is pray for them, right?"

His gaze slid away. "Right."

Johanna poured the broth mixture into the pan with the shallots. She couldn't remember ever feeling so relaxed in a man's company.

She stirred the sauce, watching it thicken, then added in a generous amount of heavy cream. "This is pretty much ready now, so you can move over to the table."

"It smells insanely good." He got up and walked to the dining table, grabbing a seat.

"Let's hope it tastes as good." She served the steaks on two plates, pouring the sauce over each and adding a sprinkle of fresh chives.

Gunnar sniffed appreciatively as she set a plate in front of him.

"Shall we give thanks?" Johanna brought a bowl of salad to the table, then sat opposite him.

He nodded, and she bowed her head. "Thank you, Lord, for this meal and all your good gifts to us. Amen."

Johanna sliced into her steak. Yes! It was a perfect medium rare.

Gunnar shook his head as he chewed his first bite. "Unbelievably good. How did you learn to cook like this?" The expression on his face was the best compliment ever.

She grinned. "Thank you. I don't know, cooking is just my happy place." She turned to where Cleo lay on the sofa. "Sorry, Cleo, but I just love making people food more than cat treats."

She faced Gunnar again. "Thanks for allowing me the space to figure it out on my own."

Then it hit her. That's what was different about Gunnar. Around him, she felt no pressure to fit into a particular box. She wasn't constantly trying to read his interests or gage his mood so she could know what role she should play. What had Reidun said about her dating habits? *When you like a guy, Johanna, you tend to let his every whim guide your decisions. Your boyfriend says jump and you go out and buy a trampoline.*

Wait. Did she like Gunnar that way? Why did her mind even go there? Now she was going to ruin a lovely evening by policing her actions and words and worrying about what he thought of her.

Her mouth went dry, and she put her fork down.

His gaze focused on her. "Is something the matter?"

"No." She shook her head. Maybe if she kept the conversation going, it'd keep her mind too busy for any more dumb thoughts. "So, I've always wondered. What brought you up here to Berghaven? Usually the relocation traffic goes one way."

He closed his eyes briefly, then looked at her again. "I needed to get away from Trondheim."

A nervous laugh escaped. "You're not a criminal or anything, are you?"

"Not in the legal sense. But I did something really bad a couple of years ago."

What could solid, straight-as-an-arrow Gunnar have possibly done? "Did you get a parking fine or something?"

He didn't smile at her feeble attempt at a joke. "Are you sure you want to know? It's not a pretty story."

She swallowed. "Most true stories aren't."

He closed his eyes for a moment, then started to talk. "My family used to be very close. So, we were all excited when my brother got serious with a girl. Her name was Annette."

He said the name as though it left a bad taste in his mouth.

"Stefan was talking about proposing, and we all liked her when he brought her home to meet us. She was interested in Christianity and started coming over to our church. Pappa was the head pastor, and I was a deacon and ran the outreach ministry for people who wanted to know more about what it means to be a Christian. We had some good talks about faith, the Bible, Jesus.

"A few months after we'd met her, she said she wanted to give her life to the Lord, and I prayed with her. Stefan wasn't a believer—he still isn't—but he joked that he had no problem marrying a nice Christian girl because they made good wives.

"She still had lots of questions and my first mistake was taking it upon myself to be her mentor. At first, we mainly talked about faith. And then she started confiding in me about things in her past. Instead of referring her to my father or someone in the women's ministry, or even my brother, who was her boyfriend, I continued meeting up with her to counsel her and be a shoulder to cry on. I started to have feelings for her. And she began to wonder whether she should break up with Stefan now that she was a Christian and he wasn't."

"Oh, no," Johanna whispered. Her sinking heart suspected where the story was going.

Gunnar's gaze dropped. "One evening, I stupidly decided to meet her at my place. For 'counseling.' A strong, spiritual guy like me was above temptation, right?" His face twisted. "Wrong. We crossed a line. A very big line. And then my brother found out. He was furious with both of us, of course, me especially. He broke up with her. I was sick with guilt over what we'd done, and I thought the best way to make things right was to marry Annette."

Johanna's breath caught in her throat. He hadn't been joking. This wasn't a pretty story at all.

Gunnar pushed a trembling hand through his hair. "I proposed to her, and we planned a rushed wedding. I didn't want to tear my family apart over whether to come or not, so Annette and I were going to get married at the registry office. The morning we were supposed to go, I went to pick her up, and she wasn't there. She'd left a note with her roommate, saying she couldn't go through with the wedding."

He scrubbed his hand down his face. "That's when reality hit me. I'd sinned against God by sleeping with a woman who wasn't my wife. I'd betrayed my brother by sleeping with his girlfriend. I'd torn my family apart. And now she'd dumped me, so it was all for nothing. The scandal nearly destroyed our church. All the people I'd talked to about Jesus—"

He pushed away from the table and got to his feet abruptly, then walked toward the window. Fists clenched, he leaned his forehead against the glass pane.

Johanna sat frozen in her chair, her gaze riveted on Gunnar.

His eyes were red-rimmed when he turned to face her. "That's the worst part of it—the people to whom I've given reason to despise the gospel. Most of all, my brother." He drew in a ragged breath, squeezing his eyes shut.

There were no words of wisdom she could share. No hollow platitudes that could paper over his pain. And he should be feeling pain—his actions had hurt so many people.

"How is Stefan now?" she asked.

Anguish washed over his face. "Angry. Bitter. And I deserve it. I've been reaching out all this time, but he wouldn't take my calls. The last time we met, he punched me in the face. So, I've kept out of the way and haven't gone to any family gatherings if I know he's going to be around. I visit my parents' home like a thief in the night, all of us holding our breath and hoping Stefan won't pop in unannounced.

"But last week, the day of your barbecue, he replied to my email. My sister is organizing an anniversary party for our parents. It's actually going to be tomorrow. Mamma wants all of us to come, but I couldn't see how. I haven't been in the same room as Stefan in years. I didn't want to just show up and cause a scene and ruin what might be my parents' last anniversary together. But Stefan said he was willing to put his feelings aside so I can attend the party."

"That's good news."

He looked at her with a thin smile. "You asked me why I moved to Berghaven. When Lukas was sick last year and asked whether I could come over here and help him out with his business, I leaped at the chance. Maybe it was the coward's way out, but I was desperate to leave town. Does that answer your question?"

"And then some." She stared at him. "You've been carrying that all this time?"

"I don't want you to feel sorry for me. Most of it is self-inflicted."

"But not your mother's illness."

He gripped the back of the sofa. "No, not that. But at least she'll have that anniversary party, whatever happens afterwards."

He was silent for a long moment, staring at his hands.

"Gunnar."

He looked up at her.

"You're a good man."

His eyes glistened.

"It's true," she said, getting up from her chair and walking closer to him. "You made a horrible mistake, the kind of blunder that only God can clean up. But you are a good man."

He bowed his head, brushing at his eyes with the back of his hand.

She stood next to him and slid her arms around him. He turned his body toward her, holding her tightly as she leaned her head against his shoulder.

Chapter 26

HER KINDNESS ALMOST UNDID him. Gunnar fought to pull himself back from dissolving into a slobbering, weeping heap as Johanna hugged him. He couldn't allow the trickle of tears to turn into a flood.

Taking slow, deliberate breaths, he gained back a measure of control.

He allowed himself to hold her for one more moment, savoring the fragrance of her hair, the way she fit so perfectly in his arms. Then he released her gently, taking a few steps across the room.

She looked up at him, her brown eyes filled with a soft light. Did she know the effect she had on him?

He cleared his throat, but his voice was still husky. "I'm not sure what to say now."

"That makes two of us. I threw out the script a while ago, and I'm just winging it."

He sighed. "Johanna, you're a lovely person. But I—"

"No, don't." She held up her hand, her color deepening. "This script, I do know. You're sorry, you don't want me to get the wrong impression, and you're not looking for a relationship right now. It's okay—I get it."

"That's not it at all." The expression on her face shot a shard of ice through his heart. He couldn't let her think he was rejecting her, although he needed to push her away. He took a step toward her. "There's nothing I'd like more than to spend more time with you, get to know you better, and see where it might lead. Do you know how insanely amazing you are?"

"Not really, no."

"Well, you are. I have no idea how some lucky man hasn't already found you. I wish it could be me, but I need to work on myself before I'm in any shape to be the man you deserve. I wasn't expecting to feel like this now, to stumble into someone like you, when I have so much I still need to work through. I don't have the right to ask you, but if I did, is there a chance you could see me like that?"

Her eyes glistened. "Yes. Cleo figured out you were a pretty cool guy long before I did." She tried for a smile, but her lips trembled. "I'm not sure I'm in a great place emotionally, either. I've just learned some hard truths about myself and my own relationship patterns. I probably shouldn't jump straight into anything without talking to someone a lot wiser than I am and praying about it a lot. I don't want to mess up again."

She wrapped her arms around her body. He ached to hold her again, but he held himself back. "So what do we do?"

"I don't know. I'm not used to being smart about men."

He chuckled. "And I've just told you how dumb I've been. The dunce of the class, who probably needs to stand in the corner until he learns his lesson. Do you mind if I talk to someone about this? Lukas and Pastor Alver, I mean. I wouldn't break any confidences, of course. I'd just tell them I've met a woman I really like and I want to get to a place where I can wisely woo her if she still wants me to."

"Woo her?" she repeated. "When's the last time I heard that word? But I don't mind you talking to Lukas and Pastor Alver. I'll need to walk with a close friend, too. Bethany, for sure. And Reidun."

For the first time in ages, hope stirred in his heart. He'd assumed the rest of his life would be years of look-ing back with bitter regret. Could there actually be a dawn of hope? An undeserved second chance?

"I'd better go now. My flight to Trondheim leaves really early. I won't pray with you now. I learned with An-nette that it can create an intimacy that perhaps isn't wise at this point. But I'll be praying alone and with Lukas."

She nodded. "Okay. I'll be praying for your family, and that the party goes well."

"Thanks." With the miracles God was working, Gunnar felt hopeful about the party.

He headed to the door, then stopped with his fingers on the han-dle. "I forgot I need to take down those cat missing flyers and put the new ones in everyone's mailboxes."

Her eyes widened. "Was that this year? It feels like a long time ago. I'll take care of it. You need to get ready for your trip."

He stood at the open door, his gaze lingering on her face. Then he walked out.

Johanna's heart beat wildly as Gunnar's gaze caressed her face.

When he left, she sagged into an armchair. Her mind whirled after the roller coaster of this insane evening. Anton, Cleo, the awful couple who'd tried to hold on to her cat... it all faded in the face of Gunnar opening his past and his heart to her. And her own heart's response to his.

But their hearts had led them both astray before, and they needed to listen to their heads and pump the brakes. Maybe that's what would make the difference this time.

Although she accepted the need to take things very slowly, she could still hold on to a little seed of hope. Perhaps, with time, it would blossom into a future with Gunnar.

She clasped her hands together and prayed.

Chapter 27

GUNNAR SMILED AS HIS sister Maria waved in the arrivals lounge at Trondheim Airport, Værnes.

He was grateful she'd offered to pick him up. His mind, bouncing like a pinball between Johanna, meeting Stefan, and tonight's party, was too full to deal with the added burden of getting a rental car.

Maria greeted him with a quick hug. "Is that all your luggage?"

Gunnar nodded, looking at his garment bag and carry-on suitcase. "I'm only staying one night. How's Mamma?"

She took his garment bag. "Beyond excited. She was up half the night rearranging the family albums. I left Pappa trying to get her to rest, so she doesn't get overly tired."

He followed her to her red Toyota Yaris and settled into the passenger seat.

Maria glanced at him as she fastened her seatbelt. "Stefan is probably at Mamma and Pappa's place. He called to tell me he was on his way."

Gunnar's palms went slick as he fumbled his safety belt in place. "Does he know I'm coming?"

"Yes. I told him."

Gunnar let out a slow breath, leaning back in his seat. He'd expected to have a bit more time, but it would be better to get that first meeting with Stefan out of the way before the party. He closed his eyes, praying for wisdom and grace.

"There's something else. I think you should know that Stefan has been talking to Annette again."

"What?" Gunnar sat up with a jolt.

Maria made a face. "Yup. There's a chance she might come to the party. It's none of my business, so I didn't try to persuade him otherwise. The party's at his home, and he can invite whomever he likes."

Gunnar clenched a fist. "He's under no obligation to consider my discomfort, either, since the whole situation is my fault."

Maria threw him a sidelong glance, then turned her gaze back to the road.

Gunnar sighed. "I appreciate the heads-up."

He hadn't seen Annette since the eve of their canceled wedding. She'd called him two months after that, wanting to get back together, but he'd turned her down. How was he even supposed to behave if he saw her again?

Part of him wanted to pump Maria for information about Annette and Stefan. But it was better not to know. He was here today for Mamma and Pappa, and it was best to keep the drama to a minimum.

"How's Berghaven?" Maria asked.

"Peaceful."

They made small talk for the rest of the half hour drive to Trondheim.

Maria pulled into the driveway of their parents' modest single-storied home. A black late model Tesla gleamed next to the front yard. "Stefan's here," she said.

Tension coiled Gunnar's gut as he got out of the car. He followed Maria into the house, wheeling his suitcase behind him. Voices were coming from the living room.

Setting the bag in the entryway, Gunnar went into the living room.

His gaze landed on his brother as though dragged by a magnetic force. Stefan stood as their gazes locked.

It was like looking at himself in one of those funhouse mirrors that distorts the viewer's reflection. Stefan was broader in the chest and shoulders, and he had the added height to go with it. They had the same short brown hair and blue eyes, although Stefan's were paler. The color of ice.

Gunnar forced his feet to move forward as he scanned Stefan's face. He couldn't read his brother's expression. Stefan didn't smile, but he didn't look angry, either. Just a blank poker face.

Stefan nodded once, then averted his gaze, resuming his seat in an armchair.

Gunnar's mouth was dry, and his mind blank. For the first time, he noticed Mamma lying back in her recliner.

She held out her arms. "Gunnar, darling, I'm so glad you made it. How are you?"

"I'm good." He bent over her, heart twisting as her thin arms wrapped around his middle.

Pappa spoke from the seat beside Stefan. "I've been trying to convince her to get some rest before tonight."

"I wanted to see you boys first," Mamma said, leaning back. "Before everyone else comes, and it gets too busy to have a proper conversation."

Pappa walked up to her and placed a hand on her shoulder. He looked up, first at Stefan, then at Gunnar. "It means a lot to us that you're both here. Thank you."

Gunnar stole a glance at Stefan. His brother sat leaning forward, forearms resting on his knees, his fingers clasped together.

"This is your day," Stefan said. "I want it to be special for you."

"It is," Mamma said. "Gunnar, how was your flight from Berghaven?"

"Uneventful. That's how I like it."

Stefan turned toward him. "You're living in Berghaven now? Isn't that really far north?"

"Yes, it's in Finnmark."

"I've never been north of Tromsø. What's it like up there?"

Was he actually making small talk with Stefan? He matched his brother's casual tone in the same way he would if having a polite conversation with a stranger. "It's beautiful. The most striking thing is there are no trees, but I soon got used to it."

"When did you move?"

Gunnar hesitated. He'd moved eleven months after Annette stood him up at the altar. That was, nine months after she tried to get back into his life and a couple of weeks after Stefan socked him in the face. "About a year, maybe."

"Sweetheart, you really must get some proper rest," Pappa said.

Gunnar followed his father's gaze to Mamma's face. Her eyes fluttered open. She must have fallen asleep on the recliner.

She yawned, her wedding and engagement rings hanging loosely over the frail hand that covered her mouth. "Okay, okay. I'll go to bed."

She pushed herself up and reached for the walker that stood next to the recliner.

Stefan stepped forward. "No, I'll help."

He swept her up in his arms as though she weighed little more than a child. A lead weight settled on Gunnar's heart as Stefan carried their mother out of the living room. How much longer did Mamma have?

He got up, desperate for some fresh air. "I'm going to the backyard."

"I'll come, too," Maria said.

They walked into the garden. It looked impeccable, as always. Pappa was a keen gardener and found a sense of peace tending his plants. Gunnar breathed in the scent of lavender.

Maria stepped up beside him. "That seemed to go okay."

He didn't have to ask what she meant. "At least he didn't punch me. That's progress, I guess. But I wish I knew what he's thinking."

She shrugged. "You know what he's like. He's a closed book."

Gunnar faced the shed which held Pappa's gardening tools. "Remember when we were kids, and we tried to build a time machine in the shed?"

"Yes." Maria chuckled. "Mamma wondered why we were collecting all those bottle caps."

"And when we told her they were to power up its magma neutron core, she started asking all the neighbors and people from church to give us their bottle caps. We needed, what was it, one hundred of them to reach warp speed?"

"Two hundred."

Gunnar and Maria whirled around.

Stefan had come up so quietly that Gunnar hadn't heard him. Stefan nodded toward the shed. "It took two hundred bottle caps to get the magma neutron core to warp one. Warp one could move us five hundred years into the past or the future."

"How many did we collect in the end?" Maria asked.

"Four hundred," Stefan said. "We didn't want to get stuck in the past."

Gunnar's breath caught in his throat. Did Stefan mean his words to have a double meaning? Was he trying to say he was willing to move on from what Gunnar had done?

But Stefan was staring at the shed, and Gunnar dared not assume his brother meant anything more than the literal meaning of his words.

"I remember," Maria said. "Where did we go in the end?" Being the youngest, it wasn't surprising that she had the foggiest memory of those days.

Stefan stroked his chin. "I think we went to the siege of Constantinople. And you got kidnapped and Gunnar and I had to storm the fort to bust you out."

Maria grinned. "We had some great times here."

A spasm of emotion crossed over Stefan's face, but it was gone before Gunnar could read it.

Stefan sighed. "I'd better get back home. There's lots to do before tonight."

"I'll join you in about an hour," Maria said.

"Okay." He turned and nodded at Gunnar. "See you later."

Maria stood next to Gunnar as Stefan made his way back to the house. When he was inside, she turned back to Gunnar and spoke in a low voice. "Thank God, that seemed to go okay. What did you think?"

Gunnar held up his hands, palms outward. "I'm amazed. I really wasn't expecting him to be so chilled out." It was too early to expect trust and friendship to fully return, but at least Stefan was being civil.

"Let's pray tonight goes without a hitch," Maria said. "You need to bring Mamma and Pappa over for half-past five to make sure she's settled before the rest of the guests arrive at six. I think it'll be best to bring her wheelchair so she doesn't have to navigate the walker around. Pappa knows how to set it all up."

"Okay. Anything else that needs doing in the meantime?"

"Maybe make sure Pappa gets a couple of hours' rest, too. And... pray."

Gunnar remembered there was a chance Annette might attend the party tonight. He'd definitely be praying.

Maria squeezed his arm. "Don't worry. You've got this."

Chapter 28

GUNNAR'S CHEST TIGHTENED AS Pappa adjusted Mamma's pillows, the older man's wrinkled, large-knuckled hands as tender as a mother with a newborn child. Pappa kissed her forehead as she settled in a chaise longue that was set up as the focal point in Stefan's large garden.

The party decorator had gone wild with a gold and white color palette and an unlimited allowance of balloons, flowers, streamers, and fairy lights. The effect was magical.

But the real magic was in his parents' faces. Mamma's face glowed, and his father's eyes reflected her delight. The hair and makeup artist Maria hired had touched up Mamma's skin to mask her pallor, but the radiance that lit her up came from within.

Gunnar swallowed the painful lump in his throat. What did it take to come through fifty years of marriage and still look at each other with joy and tenderness, despite Mamma's cancer-ravaged body and the natural toll of time on both of them?

Certainly not what Gunnar had with Annette—furtive, stolen moments of illicit passion built on a foundation of lies and betrayal.

Would the spark he and Johanna had just discovered go the distance?

A sound behind him broke into his thoughts. Gunnar turned to see Stefan standing with his arms folded.

Stefan spoke to their mother. "The guests will start arriving soon. Are you comfortable? Warm enough?"

Mamma smiled. "Yes, I'm fine. This place looks so beautiful. I can't believe you've gone through so much trouble."

"It might be good to have an extra blanket," Pappa said, stroking Mamma's hand. "Just in case the breeze picks up."

Stefan nodded. "Gunnar, if you'll come with me, I'll give you a blanket to bring back."

Gunnar followed Stefan into the house. They walked past the wide open-plan kitchen, now a beehive of bustling caterers and wait staff, and down the hall.

Stefan led him into a large home office, and Gunnar frowned. This wasn't where he'd have expected his brother to keep his extra blankets.

Stefan gestured at an armchair in front of the massive glass-topped desk. "Please sit down. I'd like to talk to you for a moment."

Gunnar sat, his senses suddenly on edge.

"This won't take long." Stefan closed the door and walked around his desk, settling into the throne-like wingback leather chair. He rested his elbows on the desk and stared down at Gunnar, his eyes like chips of ice. "Annette and I are back together."

Gunnar swallowed. "Maria mentioned that."

"Did she?" Stefan's eyes narrowed. "So, you've been talking about us."

Gunnar shook his head. "She just wanted to give me a heads-up so I wouldn't be surprised if Annette was here today."

Stefan's face darkened. "I see. Because, of course, Gunnar's comfort comes first. Every awkward wrinkle must be smoothed out ahead of time to make things as easy as possible for you."

What was that supposed to mean? Was Stefan trying to provoke him? Gunnar clenched his fists until his nails bit into the flesh of his palms.

He forced his hands to relax. He could allow his brother a few free jabs.

This was difficult for all of them, especially Stefan. Gunnar let the comment go. "Congratulations. I wish you both the best."

Stefan's lip curled. "Thanks."

Gunnar began to get up from his seat. With Stefan's current mood, nothing good was going to come out of this talk.

Stefan raised a hand. "Wait. I'm not done yet."

Gunnar lowered himself into the chair.

Stefan glared at him. "I want you to know that the only reason I'm tolerating you in my house is because of Mamma. If it wasn't for how much this party means to her and Pappa, I would never have allowed scum like you anywhere near my home. Annette told me what you did to her."

A chill swept over Gunnar. "What I did to her?" he echoed. Was his brother delusional?

Stefan's lips trembled. "You're trying to play innocent? Why do you even bother when everyone knows what a hypocrite you are?"

His brother's words hit Gunnar like a punch to the gut. "I know I made a terrible mistake. And I'll never stop being sorry for that."

"Oh, yes, the repentance spiel." Stefan spoke through gritted teeth. "You Christians love that. You get to be welcomed back into the fold like a poor little lamb that went astray. You slammed a wrecking ball into my life, but never mind, all's forgiven and you can go your merry way and attend Mamma and Pappa's anniversary like the golden boy who can do no wrong. But they don't know the full story."

Something wasn't tracking here. Even as the venom of Stefan's tirade spilled out like corrosive acid, Gunnar sensed a level of rage deeper than anything his brother had ever shown.

Gunnar raised both hands. "Wait. What full story?"

"You can stop lying, big brother." Spittle flecked Stefan's lips as he spat out the words. "It's over. Annette just told me how you forced yourself on her and then tried to blackmail her into marrying you."

The air rushed out of Gunnar's lungs. What madness was this?

"That's right," Stefan snarled. "I know everything. I already thought you were despicable, but that's beyond evil. You're a predator and you deserve to be in prison for what you did. Annette trusted you. You were this holy deacon, and you tricked her into coming into your house for so-called 'spiritual counseling'. The only reason she didn't tell the police about your abuse is she was worried it would break Mamma's heart. She didn't even want me to know, but she finally broke down and told me."

Gunnar's mind reeled. He scrabbled to find a handhold, something from this slick impenetrable wall of lies on which he could hang a denial.

Stefan's eyes burned with loathing. "You owe Mamma a lot. If it wasn't for her, you'd be dead to me. In fact, you are dead to me. As far as I'm concerned, I don't have a brother. As soon as this party is over, I never want to lay eyes on you again. Stay away from me and my fiancée. I'm done. Now, get out."

"Stefan, whatever Annette has told you—"

"Get out!" Stefan's face turned purple as his yell echoed off the walls of the room.

Gunnar rose to his feet, staring at his brother's contorted features.

Stefan's hands curled into fists. "And to think I was considering forgiving you earlier today. You make me sick."

Gunnar stumbled toward the door. There was no point in saying anything more. Stefan would never believe him. He had already betrayed his brother. It wasn't surprising that Stefan was willing to accept whatever lies Annette had told him.

He stepped out into the hallway. A movement in the corner of his vision made him turn his head. Someone was standing at the top of the stairs. His gaze collided with a petite woman with blond hair cropped in a pixie cut. His body recoiled with the same instinctive revulsion as if he'd stepped on a scorpion.

Annette stared down at him, her red lips twisted into a smirk. Her features, as perfect as a china doll, hadn't changed. But how had he ever found her beautiful? She held his gaze, then turned her back on him, hips swaying slowly as she walked around a corner.

Chapter 29

GUNNAR STEADIED HIMSELF AGAINST the wall, staring up the stairs where Annette had leered at him like a malevolent phantom from his past.

It all began to make sense, coming together like the pieces of a nightmarish puzzle. Stefan's re-ignited fury, those repugnant accusations, Annette's presence in his house. She'd filled his brother's mind with poison and lies. Like the most deadly lies, there was enough truth mixed in to mask the taste of the deception.

Gunnar had seen himself as Annette's mentor and spiritual counselor. He was in a position of authority as a deacon. And he had succumbed to his desire for her, knowing it was sinful, and that Stefan wanted to propose to her.

This new story of him coercing her into his bed and trying to force her to marry him—that was a complete lie. But when he was already guilty of so much, all she'd had to do was give Stefan a nudge to make him believe the rest.

Why now? Why here at his parents' anniversary party, when every moment with Mamma was a priceless treasure? Did Annette hate him that much? Nobody's heart could be that dark.

He walked back toward the back-yard, bumping into a waiter in the kitchen.

A tray load of glasses smashed onto the tiled floor.

Gunnar stared at the mess, then at the waiter's horrified face. "I'm so, so, sorry."

The catering manager came bustling forward. Gunnar pulled out his wallet and extracted a business card, which he shoved into the manager's hands. "Here. Maria hired you—I'm her brother. Please send me an invoice for the damage. I'm really sorry."

He broke away from her torrent of words, desperate to get outside.

Guests had already started arriving. He was going to have to talk to people, smile at people, make casual chitchat while knowing his brother hated him, thanks to the vile lies of a woman Gunnar had once thought he loved.

He jumped as something touched his arm.

"Hey, are you okay? You don't look very well." Maria peered into his face. "You're not coming down with something, are you?"

Gunnar shook his head. He glanced around. Guests milled around the garden, but he saw no sign of Annette or Stefan. He stepped closer to Maria, pitching his voice below the hum of the guests and the gentle strains of low key jazz. "Stefan told me he and Annette are back together."

Maria blinked at him. "Is that a problem?"

"It shouldn't be. But she's told him a disgusting lie about me, and he believes her. He hates me."

"What? No! What did she say?"

Gunnar shook his head. "I don't even want to repeat it, but it's foul, and it's a complete lie. But Stefan thinks it's true." His eyes stung. "The only thing I want right now is for Mamma to enjoy her day. I'm not going to say or do anything to take away from that. As soon as I can, I'm going to get an Uber, collect my stuff, and go back to Berghaven. Will you drive Mamma and Pappa back home?"

Tears filled Maria's eyes as she nodded.

Her expression wrung Gunnar's heart. This should have been a happy day for her, as well as their parents.

She'd put so much into organizing this party. She, too, was collateral damage to his blunders.

"I'm sorry to bring you into this," he said. "Can you try to carry on as though nothing has changed? At least for tonight."

"You're not going to let her get away with whatever she's saying, though, are you?"

Gunnar rubbed his temples. "I don't know. My head is going to explode. I need to think of just one thing at a time right now, and all that matters is making sure Mamma and Pappa have only good memories about tonight."

He closed his eyes as the music and hum of conversation washed around them.

Maria's fingers closed around his arm in a vice-like grip. "Stefan's just come outside with Annette. I think it might be best if you slip away now. I'll tell Mamma and Pappa you're not feeling well. That's not a lie, anyway."

Gunnar looked up, following Maria's gaze. Stefan stood next to Annette, his arm around her slender shoulders, holding her close to him.

Gunnar dragged his gaze away. The sight of Annette sheltered in his brother's protective arm made him physically ill. Maria would definitely not be lying about him feeling unwell. "Thanks. I'll call an Uber."

She gave his arm a farewell squeeze. He skirted around the edge of the garden, making for the front of the house.

In the driveway, he pulled out his cell phone. He had several text messages, but he zeroed in on the one from Johanna.

Hey! Just wanted you to know I'm praying for you. Did it go okay meeting your brother? How's the party going? Looking forward to hearing about it when you get back.

Dear, sweet Johanna. He was twice an idiot. A fool for letting her into his heart, and an even bigger fool for thinking he could build a relationship with her. Was there anyone he loved whom he hadn't hurt? How could he involve her in this sickening mess?

His thumb hovered over the screen as her kind words tortured him. He punched the delete icon.

Chapter 30

"JOHANNA STRAND, IF YOU look at your phone one more time, I'm going to grab it from you, find your ugliest selfie, and text it to a random number in your address book."

Johanna tore her gaze away from her phone screen and glanced at Reidun. "Okay, okay. I'm sorry."

The friends were hiking on a trail that ran parallel to the fjord. Their weekly walk after church was a time both of them valued as a chance to talk. It was even more precious now that they were the only single women left in their friendship group, and Johanna was flouting their no-screens rule.

She stuffed the phone into her pants pocket.

"Who are you so desperate to hear from, anyway?" Reidun asked.

Johanna sighed. "Gunnar. He's not replied to any of my messages since yesterday afternoon."

"Of course." Much of today's hike had been spent with Johanna filling Reidun in on her budding relationship with her neighbor. "Isn't he still in Trondheim? Maybe he's busy with family stuff."

Johanna kicked a tuft of scrub. "He came back last night. I saw his car pulling in and I know he's at home. I

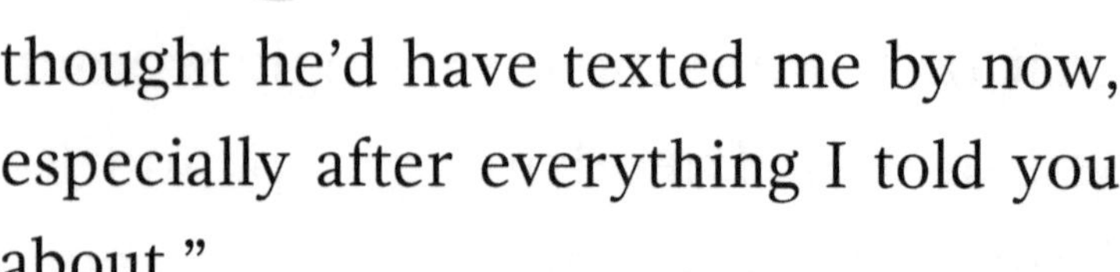

thought he'd have texted me by now, especially after everything I told you about."

"Oh."

They walked for a few moments.

Reidun stopped and faced her friend. "Go and talk to him."

"Are you serious?"

"Yes." Reidun folded her arms. "You said you wanted to do this relationship differently, right? You want to be mature and grown up without being coy and waiting for phone calls and text messages that will never come."

"I'm scared of coming across like a stalker, though, and pushing him away. If he wanted to get in touch, wouldn't he have done it by now?"

"You have a point." Reidun rubbed her chin.

They walked for a minute, then Reidun stopped again. "Hold on. What did you just say?"

"I said if Gunnar wanted to get in touch, he'd have done it by now."

"No, before that. You said you're scared of pushing him away."

Johanna nodded. "Yes. And?"

"If you're worried about Gunnar, instead of being concerned about pushing him away, maybe your first concern should be to check whether he actually needs something right now. What if he's burning up with a fever or lying unconscious with a concussion? Don't guess about what might or might not offend him. That's putting the focus on yourself and your own fears of rejection. Reach out the same

way you'd reach out to me if I'd gone radio silent."

Johanna stared at her friend. "You think I'm more worried about offending him and how that might impact on me?"

"That's putting it very baldly, but yes. I've had ringside seats to your previous relationships. You've tied yourself up in so many knots because you were scared of pushing your boyfriends away. Need I remind you of your closetful of hobbies to get your boyfriends to stick around?"

"Ouch." Reidun was right. Johanna spoke slowly. "Okay. I'll stop being scared about pushing him away like a boyfriend I want to cling onto, and think instead of what he might need. Like a friend."

"Just drop by and ask how he's doing. You're his neighbor. Visit with a pie or something."

Johanna knocked on Gunnar's front door a few hours later. She didn't bring a pie, but a freshly baked *fyrstekake*. The short crust cake with fragrant marzipan filling was supposed to be for festive occasions, but it was one of Johanna's specialties.

Gunnar pulled open the door, threading his fingers through his hair.

Johanna's heart skipped a beat. He didn't look very happy to see her. She held up her pie dish. "Congratulations on your parents' fiftieth anniversary."

His lips tilted upward. "I love *fyrstekake*. Thank you." He took the cake from her and stood aside. "You'd better come in."

Johanna stepped across the threshold. It was the first time she'd been inside Gunnar's home. The large windows would have allowed in plenty of natural light if they hadn't been shuttered.

His home was uncluttered and orderly, making the carry-on suitcase in the hallway and crumpled suit jacket on the floor seem out of place. Hadn't he unpacked since yesterday?

Gunnar put the cake on the coffee table. He pulled open the vertical blinds in front of the large window that looked out onto the fjord.

Light streamed in, exposing his haggard features as he turned to face her. "I owe you an explanation. You're probably wondering why I've been so quiet."

"The thought did cross my mind." She sat on an armchair. "Are you okay?"

"Not really, no." The tremor in his voice set her on edge.

He sat opposite her, interlocking his hands on top of his head. Turning his face toward the ceiling, he blinked rapidly, as though to hold tears at bay.

Johanna's stomach churned. "What's wrong? Is it your mother?"

"No, she's as well as could be expected. She had a wonderful time. I don't think she suspected anything was wrong. At least I can be thankful for that."

He lowered his hands, balling them into fists. "When I met Stefan, it went better than I'd expected at first. He was cold, but polite. He's seeing Annette again."

Johanna's chest tightened. Was this why Gunnar was so upset?

He cleared his throat. "Then a couple of hours later, everything changed. They must have talked. When I saw Stefan again, he was enraged. Hateful. Annette told him that I—" he flinched, swallowing hard, and dragged his hand across his mouth. "She told him I assaulted her and forced her to sleep with me, then blackmailed her into agreeing to marry me."

A wave of revulsion hit Johanna. What kind of woman would lie about something like that? "Did he believe her?"

"Yes." An entire cosmos of anguish filled the small word.

"I'm so sorry."

He leaned his head against the sofa, closing his eyes. A tear trickled down the side of his face.

She moved to his side, wrapping her arms around him. He turned toward her and she cradled him with her body as his raw, guttural sobs ripped through her. This was a pain beyond what she could fathom. She held on until her arms ached, willing them to hang on longer and speak comfort her words could not form. His anguish,

laid bare, belonged to her, and she rocked slowly back and forth.

Gunnar felt like he was drowning in a bottomless well of sorrow. Gasping for air, he clung on to Johanna as the agony engulfed him. The burden of his guilt crushed his heart and racked his soul with relentless waves of pain.

He knew his sin was forgiven, but he grieved for the harm he had caused, the wounds that might never be repaired. Even Annette's malicious lies would have had no power if he hadn't fueled them with his initial act.

As he wept, his heart cried out a desperate prayer for God to heal that which his sin had broken.

The flow of his grief began to subside, and Gunnar loosened his hold on Johanna. Moving back, he rasped a breath and gathered her hands in his, holding them against his heart.

He closed his eyes, praying again as his breath slowed down, then gazed at her face. Her brown eyes were red-rimmed and damp with tears, her makeup smudged, but she had never looked so beautiful.

He groped for the right words, praying that she would hear his heart. "Your coming here to me was so sweet and precious. You have no idea what you've done. Thank you." He squeezed her hands, his voice roughening.

She returned the pressure, her eyes filling up again.

"But I need to be alone right now, to pray and seek wisdom and figure things out. I think I know what I have to do, but I need to be sure. I promise to tell you when I am. Do you understand?"

She nodded.

He placed her hands gently in her lap, then let them go. "Thank you. For everything."

They both stood, and she brushed her fingers across her eyes. "I'll be praying for you," she said, then turned and walked to the door.

Chapter 31

JOHANNA ONLY KNEW SHE'D fallen asleep when she woke up the next morning. She reached for her phone, searching for any message from Gunnar. There was none.

Was he okay? The intensity of his pain had scared her, and she still didn't know whether she'd done the right thing. She'd just acted on instinct, reaching out to comfort him. She bowed her head, lifting up another prayer for him as he wrestled with whatever decisions he had to make.

She climbed out of bed and stumbled into the bathroom. It was Monday morning. Thank goodness she didn't need to go anywhere or see anyone.

She took a long shower, then dressed in light blue jogging pants and a matching hoodie.

As she walked into the kitchen, the doorbell rang. Her heart thundering, she ran to answer it.

Gunnar, his hair damp from his own shower, stood on her doorstep with Cleo in his arms. He smiled at her and, although there were dark smudges under his eyes, she sensed a peace radiating from him.

"Look who spent the night," he said, and bent down to put Cleo on the floor.

"I wondered where she'd gone," Johanna said. "I'm glad she was with you and not back with that gruesome twosome."

The shadow of a smile crossed his lips as he ran a hand through his hair. "Can we talk?"

"Yes, of course."

They went into her living room. She sat down, but he paced in front of the French windows, his hands in his pockets.

She swallowed hard, tension mounting.

Finally, he turned to face her. "I was up most of the night thinking and praying. I hope Bethany will forgive me because I called and bothered Lukas at a ridicuous hour."

He held her gaze for a long moment. "I'm moving back to Trondheim."

The air rushed from her lungs, and she felt herself sagging in her seat. Then she chided herself. This wasn't about her. It was about what he needed to do. Hadn't she prayed he would get the clarity to figure out what to do next?

She unclenched her fists. "I'm sure your mother will be happy to have you close."

"Yes. She's one of the main reasons I'm going back. I remember what you said about your own mother's final months, and I want to be near Mamma during the time she has left. I've stayed away all this time out of remorse for what I did to my brother. I thought it was the right thing to do, to remove myself from Trondheim so he wouldn't have to see me and be constantly reminded of what I did.

"And even now, I'm afraid that my being in Trondheim will cause him pain, especially with whatever lies Annette is feeding him. But I can't let that control me. I'm not going to live cowering in guilt anymore. Not when Mamma and Pappa need my support."

He walked closer and sat opposite her. "But that's not the hardest thing. I'm torn about going because it means being so far away from you just when... Johanna, I don't know what your thoughts are about us. But I know I want you in my life. You're becoming dearer to me every day. I don't know what I'd have done without your friendship over the past weeks."

Her heart sang as he took hold of her hands. "I feel the same way."

"You do? Thank God." His eyes misted up. "I know the timing and the distance isn't ideal. In fact, it's down-right rubbish. But could we try to see where this will go?"

She laughed. "Our timing definitely stinks. We're at loggerheads for months when you live next door, and now we're going to start a relationship when you're moving almost a thousand miles away."

He grinned. "Why live a simple life when you can have a complicated one?"

He moved next to her and his eyes darkened as he cupped her face in his hands.

She closed her eyes, savoring the sweetness of his lips on hers. Her arms slipped around him as he deepened the kiss, her heart hammering like it would explode.

He caressed her cheek, murmuring against her hair, "What did I do to deserve you?"

Finally, he pulled away, his hands on her shoulders. "I need to go. I have a lot to sort out with Lukas at the office and telling my parents I'm moving."

"When will you leave for Trondheim?"

"As soon as I've arranged all the logistics. There's a flight this evening. I don't know how long I'll stay, but I'll

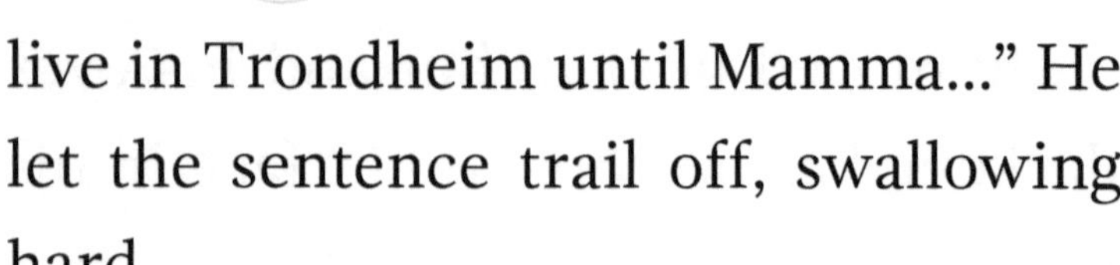

live in Trondheim until Mamma…" He let the sentence trail off, swallowing hard.

"Is there anything I can do?"

"You're already doing it." He traced a thumb across her cheek, the smoldering fire in his blue eyes melting her heart. "You're the one bright ray in my life. I'm already asking so much of you when I can offer so little right now with everything that's going on."

Her throat tightened. She had waited her whole life for him. Even though they'd found each other in the middle of a time of upheaval, she would wait as long as it took.

Chapter 32

Six Months Later

GUNNAR PUT THE LAST of his suitcases into the trunk of Maria's red Yaris and slammed the lid shut.

Although the blistering cold January wind sliced through him, he lingered for a moment, looking at his childhood home. It had been priceless to spend the last few months of Mamma's life back here, living under the same roof, supporting his father with the burden of care and grief.

He pulled his coat closer around him. So many beautiful memories had been made in this space. The contours of the house were the same, and he treasured every one of them, but it was no longer home.

He stepped inside. Johanna and Maria stood in the hallway, coats on, ready for the drive to the airport.

They both turned toward him when he entered. Johanna came to his side and slipped her arms around him.

He brushed his lips against her hair, his eyes misting. He was so glad Mamma got to meet Johanna. She'd come to spend Christmas and, as he'd suspected, the two women had loved each other on sight, their bond deepening in the cruelly short time they'd shared together.

In all the months Gunnar had stayed in Trondheim, it had been surprisingly easy to avoid Stefan and Annette. Whenever they came to visit, Gunnar stayed in his room or left the house, ceding the space to them.

After that beautiful final Christmas, Mamma had faded quickly. Johanna stayed on through Mamma's funeral in mid-January, and now they were going back to Berghaven.

"Is everything loaded up?" Maria asked.

Gunnar nodded. "Have you seen Pappa?"

"I'm here."

Pappa walked into the room, cellphone in his hand. "I was just making a couple of calls. So, you're headed for the airport?" He looked at Gunnar and Johanna.

Gunnar's heart twisted. Would Pappa be all right? Although the older man had insisted it was unnecessary, Maria had moved back into the house. She and Gunnar suspected that if Pappa were left alone, the pain of Mamma's passing would overwhelm him. His life had revolved around caring for Mamma, and the void she had left would weigh on him.

"Yes, we're ready," Gunnar said. "Maybe you and Maria can come over to Berghaven for Easter."

"We'll talk about it." Pappa glanced at his phone, then stuffed it into his pocket. "I hope you have a safe trip. It's been wonderful meeting you, Johanna." He kissed her on the forehead.

Maria shouldered her purse. "We'd better get going. There's a storm coming and I want to be back home before it hits."

They moved toward the doorway, and Gunnar caught Pappa checking his phone again.

They stepped outside, and Gunnar's heart hammered as Stefan's black Tesla pulled into the driveway.

He exchanged a look with Johanna. They walked quickly to Maria's car, his hand resting on the small of her back. They'd have to leave now if they wanted to avoid a confrontation.

Gunnar opened the door for Johanna to get into the car and was about to slip in after her when Stefan called out his name.

Gunnar's heart pounded as he glanced at Johanna's wide-eyed face. "Stay here." He wanted her far away from any ugliness.

He braced himself as he turned around to face his brother.

Stefan stepped toward him, hands stuffed into his pockets. He looked haggard, with deep lines etched on his face. "Can I have a minute?"

Their gazes met, and Gunnar was shocked to see his brother's eyes were moist.

Stefan opened his mouth to speak, his face twisting with emotion. "Let's... let's walk a bit."

Gunnar fell into step beside him, and they moved away from Maria's car, walking toward the road.

Stefan said, "Annette has gone."

"What?" Gunnar froze.

Stefan nodded, his jaw clenched. "She left me just before Mamma's funeral, but I knew long before then what a mistake I made. I didn't want to admit it to myself. It was so much easier to blame you than to face the fact that I was wrong."

"I'm so sorry." Gunnar reached out to touch his brother's arm.

Stefan flinched, but allowed the contact. "I know she lied about you. I'm still angry, and I'm not sure I can get past what I know did happen. But I know that life is short. Maybe one day, but today this is all I can do."

Gunnar's eyes filled. "I'm grateful you came."

"Pappa convinced me. And I know it's what Mamma would have wanted." He nodded toward Maria's car. Johanna's face was framed in the passenger window. "You're a very lucky man."

"I know."

They faced each other for a long moment. Finally, Stefan held out his arm. He held something inside his closed fist. "Take this."

He pressed the object into Gunnar's hand. Gunnar stared at it. It was a bottle cap. His eyes misting up, he looked at his brother's face.

Blinking quickly, Stefan walked back to his Tesla.

Tears streamed down Gunnar's face. He didn't deserve this. God was restoring his life, piece by piece.

Johanna jumped out of the car. She and Maria walked up to Gunnar as Stefan drove away.

Johanna brushed the tears from his cheeks. "Are you okay? What did Stefan say?"

His throat too choked up to speak, Gunnar stared at the bottle cap in his hand.

Maria looked at it and her hands flew to her mouth. Tears filling her eyes, she whispered, "Thank you, Jesus!"

Johanna frowned. "A bottle cap? What does that mean?"

Gunnar swallowed. "It means we shouldn't live in the past. We can visit to remember what was good, but we need to move forward."

Her face was still puzzled, but there would be plenty of time to explain. He put his arm around her shoulder. "Come on. Let's go home."

Epilogue

Six Months Later

OHANNA TOOK SEVERAL DEEP breaths to settle her nerves. No matter how many times she did it, live streaming was still stressful. The worst part was just before she started, but once she got into her groove, she knew it would be okay.

Her Table for One viewers loved her weekly "What's For Dinner" cook-along show which she streamed live on YouTube, Facebook, and Instagram. Tonight promised to be her biggest audience turnout ever.

She flexed her hands, mentally rehearsing all the steps for making Steak Diane. She'd deliberately chosen this dish to mark the one year since she'd intended to cook it for Anton, but had shared it with Gunnar instead.

And what a year it had been. Her business was flourishing beyond her craziest dreams. Thanks to Gunnar's help, she'd spread her wings beyond her YouTube channel and had a growing number of paying subscribers. She was developing a couple of online courses including one—by Reidun's request—called "Cooking for Dummies".

Johanna didn't normally have a "studio" audience for her live stream, but tonight Gunnar was in her kitchen for the filming.

A professional videography team was handling the technical stuff, so all she had to do was concentrate on cooking and connecting with her audience, like an actual chef.

Olav, the lead videographer, signaled to Johanna. "We're live in thirty seconds. Silence, please, everyone."

Gunnar gave her a thumbs up, mouthing, "You've got this."

At Olav's silent signal, Gunnar's words warming her heart, Johanna smiled at the camera. "Welcome to the Table for One live stream. I'm Johanna Strand, up in the wilds of Berghaven in northern Norway. Are you ready to cook along with me? Tonight we'll be making a three-

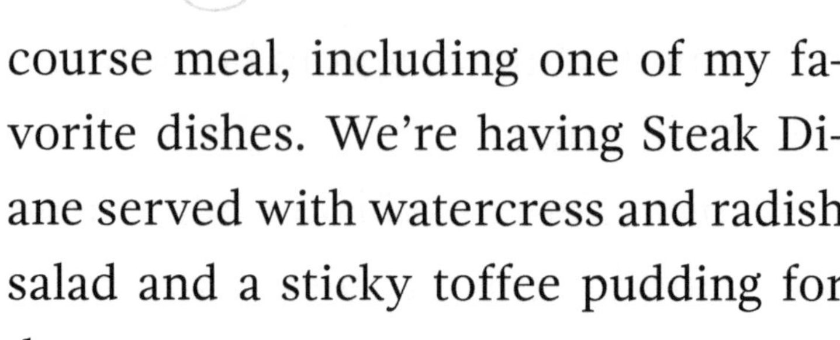

course meal, including one of my favorite dishes. We're having Steak Diane served with watercress and radish salad and a sticky toffee pudding for dessert.

"I hope you managed to grab hold of your ingredients in advance so you can cook along with me."

As she'd hoped, Johanna's nerves settled, and she began to enjoy herself, talking through the preparation of the dishes.

Gunnar walked up to her when it was over. "You did an amazing job. I'm so proud of you."

Her heart warmed at his compliment. "Thank you."

Olav and his assistants took down their equipment. As always, Johanna gave each of them a package of home-made cookies as they left the house.

When she came back to the kitchen, Gunnar was sitting at the breakfast bar.

He stood, holding out his arms.

Johanna slid into his embrace, sighing as he held her close. "I'm so relieved that's it for another week."

"Tired?"

"A bit. But I love my job."

He cradled her against his chest and she closed her eyes, listening to the steady beat of his heart.

"Why did you make Steak Diane tonight?" he asked, stroking her hair.

She smiled, her lips grazing his chest. "I had my reasons. Why do you ask?"

He brushed his hand against the side of her face. "That's what you served me that night when I first began to fall in love with you."

Her heart swelled. He understood!

Holding her closer, he kissed the top of her head. "I know it's not what either of us had planned when we had that dinner. The timing was wrong, I was an emotional wreck, my family was in crisis. I wasn't even supposed to be the one sharing that meal with you that night. But that's when it started. When I first knew that God was bringing something exquisitely beautiful amid the ashes of my life. We've come full circle. I had already planned this, but when I saw that was on your menu tonight, I knew it was perfect."

She moved back slightly, looking into his face. "What do you mean?"

Reaching into his pocket, he pulled out a small velvet box, opening it to reveal a solitaire diamond ring. "Johanna Strand, will you marry me?"

She blinked away tears. "Do I look stupid? Of course I will."

Laughing through his own tears, he slid the ring onto her finger.

She gasped. "It's so beautiful!"

"Do you think so?" He gazed into her eyes.

She nodded, too choked up to answer.

He swallowed, his eyes welling up again. "It was Mamma's. She told me on Christmas Eve that if you agree to marry me one day, she wanted you to have it."

Her heart soared on a crest of overwhelming love for him, awed at what God had done for both of them, despite their own blunders and missteps. He was truly good.

The End

Steinar is raising his son alone after losing the perfect wife. Reidun bucks traditional roles and never thought of herself as wife material, nor the mothering type. So, when they're roped in to plan their small town's Christmas festival together, the spark between them has to be a mistake. Right?

After the Frost is Book 5 in Milla Holt's *Seasons of Faith* Christian romance series. Five friends were in the same wedding in a small Norwegian town over twenty years ago. Four bridesmaids, one bride. Now, two decades on, each woman learns that God's timing is perfect as they find forever love later in life.

About the Author

I write fiction that reflects my Christian faith. I love happy endings, heroes and heroines who discover sometimes hard but always vital truths, and stories that uplift and encourage.

My family and I live in the east of England where we enjoy rambling in the countryside, reading good books and making up silly lyrics to our favorite songs.

To learn about my other books, join my mailing list, and grab a free exclusive book, visit my website at www.millaholt.com